The Ambiti  ၂

(William Gascoyne'

Royal Leamington Spa

and a changing Construction Industry)

by

Kevin Hunt

ISBN: 9798694354516

www.publishnation.co.uk

CHAPTER 1

William Gascoyne's early years

Life was never going to be easy. As the wind blew and bit every living thing it could snatch in its ever-searching appetite for victims, the white cover of freshly laid snow gave an impression of calm and peace in the yard of The Bull Inn, Stony Stratford, Buckinghamshire. The tranquillity was broken by the cries of a woman acknowledging the pain that accompanies childbirth. Elizabeth Gascoyne had provided an early present for Christmas 1827 that brought a smile of pride to her husband John's face. Their daughter Mary Ann had been their greatly loved treasure and the addition of a son could only make their Christmas a complete period of joy.

From its prominent central location, the clock tower of the parish church of St. Giles, Stony Stratford, soared high above the yard of The Bull coaching inn on the opposite side of the main road. On Christmas Day, the seasonally decorated interior of the church, with its towering fluted columns and impressive fan-vaulted ceiling, welcomed its usual large congregation. This year they were able to celebrate an additional religious ceremony as they witnessed the baptism of two babies. The first child christened was Edward Stephens, the son of a local couple. This was followed shortly after by the new Gascoyne baby who was baptised with the name William. The church service was soon followed by a joyous celebration at the Gascoyne home where family and friends were treated to the delights of Elizabeth's simple homemade food which was complemented by ale from a wooden cask provided by the landlord of The Bull Inn.

The Bull Inn was proud of its main street location and eagerly competed for business with the nearby competitor, The Cock Inn. All manner of stories was shared between the travellers as they rested and were often taken with them along the short walk between the two hostelries. As the tales were transported and retold from one inn to the other, they were often embellished and exaggerated to such a degree that they bore very little relationship to the original telling. The notoriety of this local practice is claimed to be the origin of "a cock and bull story" becoming a popular catchphrase in English society.

High Street, Stony Stratford, the market town's main thoroughfare, straddled Watling Street, the old Roman road from Chester to London and was located at a convenient distance along the route to provide a suitable resting place for weary travellers and their horses. A large number of coaching inns were established in the town to cater for the many fatigued passengers seeking a respite from the prolonged periods sitting in a horse-drawn coach fitted with a suspension system that provided limited protection from the constant pounding from the rugged road.

The Bull Inn's cobbled yard surface sloped down to a curved channel forming a drain which took a mixture of surface water and horse excrement to the rear of the yard. Large flagstones were inset between the cobbles and created a more comfortable footpath. Young William scraped his feet over the uneven cobbles of the yard while noting the activity behind each of the doors into the yard, the horses in the stables, the firelight underneath the door to Gascoyne's simple but comfortable abode. He took a drink from the wooden barrel that served as a water butt and looked out of the arched gateway where the great exciting outside world awaited. Next to the stable doors there projected a metal hook fixed securely to the brick wall on which a horse harness hung to denote the accommodation was occupied. A strong smell of fresh horse dung piled in a bucket by the door confirmed this. William glanced around in response to the sound of a mouse scurrying away beneath the wide rim wheeled wagon. It was parked at the side of the yard laden with straw ready to make a warm and comfortable bed for the weary horses at the end of a full working day.

The hipped roof dormer window from the room where William slept overlooked The Bull yard, a place where he spent endless days of great pleasure. Hours were spent running in and out of the stables which were the temporary homes of the horses that pulled the wheeled vehicles that broke their long bone-shaking journey at this popular hostelry. But his favourite doorway was the narrow aperture formed in the gable end of the annex building that projected into the yard. William helped to offset some of the rent paid by his father to the innkeeper landlord by stocking up the log piles that were stored by the inglenook fireplace. Whenever possible, William lingered as a shadowy figure in a corner of the room amid the smell of wood smoke, old beer and wet dogs, ready to stoke the fire when the burning logs had reduced to burning embers. This afforded him the opportunity to eavesdrop on the conversations of the travellers, whose many differing accents never ceased to fascinate and amuse him. William was entranced as they spoke while sitting in the winged high backed chairs in front of a roaring log fire, smoking sweet aromatic tobacco in their delicate long stemmed white clay pipes. Life in places with names such as London and Warwick were described by the travellers as they exchanged stories and news. Overhearing the travellers relaxing in the snug room of the inn captivated William's curiosity and stimulated his desire to experience this wider world.

The birth of a baby brother, James, when William was five years old, created great excitement for him and his sister. Life for William was a joy which seemed to have no bounds. Happy hours of play were mixed with his dreams of adventures to come beyond the yard archway. His first venture beyond the confines of The Bull Inn yard came with his days at school where he proved to be an able scholar who excelled in reading and writing. His alert mind marked him out as a pupil with the potential to achieve, even with the limited schooling available to him. Had he been born into a more privileged social group it is likely that he would have become a leading academic. School days seemed to fly by and William's childhood soon progressed to the early hopes and ambitions of a maturing male in a rural community.

William's first experience of the reality of how cruel life can become occurred as he approached the end of his school years. His sister speaking in whispers to the schoolmistress interrupted William's afternoon arithmetic lesson. The knowing looks in William's direction were a clear warning to him of the impending bad news. A hand gesture by the teacher summoned him to the front of the classroom.

"You are to return home with your sister immediately," instructed the teacher firmly. "You do not need to clear your desk."

As the pair walked quickly along the lane down to the main road, William was informed of his father's accident with a hay wagon which had overturned and crushed him underneath.

"Have you spoken to him?" asked William in a nervous tone.

"No," replied Mary her voice starting to crack, "I've not been allowed to be that close to him yet."

The couple when together normally engaged in almost nonstop conversation, but on this occasion the rest of their journey was conducted in total silence, as they became completely oblivious to any sounds they encountered. As they walked through the archway into the yard, the degree of seriousness became evident. A small group outside the entrance to their home fell silent as if they should not distract the attention of the new arrivals.

As they entered the room that served as both a kitchen and living room, they were met by the vicar whose opening sentence, "I'm so sorry," said everything they did not want to hear. William's mother could be heard sobbing in the adjoining room, something that he had never experienced before.

Looking at a dead body for the first time was a strange almost unreal experience. The combined facts that the body of his father was cold and motionless made the scene one which William would have emblazoned in his memory for the rest of his life. He leaned over the bed where the shell of his father lay and held out a hand to feel the cold, stone-like figure. He pulled his hand away almost embarrassed that he could no longer relate or associate with the motionless shape that was no longer his father. He could not cry and felt a degree of shame that he could not give an outward sign of the pain that he felt.

How he wished that he could follow the example of his siblings and mother in their public display of loss.

William's grief was a private affair until the day of the funeral. As the sealed coffin rested on the timber frame in front of the altar, William viewed a mental image of his father. The sensation had little effect until the vicar spoke to the congregation. As the vicar's heartfelt account of John's fruitful life and his premature demise registered with William, an inconsolable feeling of loss expressed itself in his uncontrollable sobbing. Regardless of how hard William tried to compose himself, the flood of tears continued to pour down his cheeks and soak his handkerchief. Mary stretched across with her hand and squeezed his with a firm but understanding and caring grip. This show of affection calmed his lost composure and helped William to survive the remainder of the funeral procedures without the temptation to withdraw to suffer his pain.

After the internment of the coffin in the church graveyard, the funeral party returned home. William sat in the corner listening to the members of the family comforting his mother and proposing the way forward for her. Money was short and with the lack of any income the idea of staying in Stony Stratford was out of the question. After an hour's discussion that revolved around which members of the family would be best suited to help, it was decided that those members who had travelled down from Leamington Spa offered the most promising solution. The developing spa town was a place of opportunity that had already provided a home and livelihood for four close Gascoyne relatives and their families.

"Leamington's a great town," William's cousin and namesake, William, announced. He puffed out his chest and added, "All the opportunity a young man could need. That's where he should go if you ask me."

"Leamington?" chimed in one of William's aunts. "Well my goodness. Whatever will he do there?"

"Whatever he wants," Cousin William retorted. "That's the kind of place it is." He spoke with the air of authority of someone who had been sent there as a parish apprentice to learn the trade of a hairdresser. The possibility of William following his cousin to the spa town was quickly brought into question when the general conversation turned to speculation about William's immediate future. It was apparent that his future was to be placed in the hands of the parish representatives in the hope that he too would become the subject of an apprenticeship. The location of his placement would be entirely their decision.

William's appearance before the parish representatives was a sympathetic meeting where his academic and physical skills were matched to a prestigious trade as a stonemason with a master in the capital city. William was saddened at the thought that the permanent separation from his father was to be followed so quickly by that of temporary detachment from the nub of his family. But he realised that out of the tragedy was the opportunity to enter that great wide world beyond The Bull yard's archway and the excitement of experiencing what life is like in the great metropolis. His fear and depression gave way to expectation, excitement and ambition.

CHAPTER 2

Journey to a new life in London

Packing took little time but farewell seemed to need forever. As William climbed onto the top of the coach in The Bull yard, he felt for the first time the real feeling of adventure that had he empathised with so many times as he witnessed departing travellers prepare for their journey.

His mother leaned forward and thrust the gold pocket watch that had belonged to his father into William's hand. "Never forget your family," she whispered before giving him a big hug.

"Family will always be my priority," he replied and kissed her gently on the cheek. His young brother followed the event with limited understanding, but there were tears in the eyes of his mother and sister as they handed William a piece of bread and cheese, which was to serve as lunch on his journey south to London. Their departure from the yard would follow shortly but would take them in the opposite direction.

The driver took firm grip of the reins and shouted, "Hup there," to the team of horses. The coach lurched forward on its springs and William grasped the metal rail which retained the luggage on the roof. He risked a free hand to wave to his mother and tried hard to give the impression of a smile. He felt a strange reaction in his throat and turned away before the sight could produce a breakdown of his power of control. The coach passed through the archway and turned left on the turnpike road that stretched seemingly endlessly into the distance. The small rows of cottages that lined the road gradually gave way to hedgerows and trees on either side that enclosed fertile fields.

William somehow found comfort in the sound of clattering horse hooves as they progressed along the unfamiliar highway. As the coach approached settlements both big and small, the coachman issued a warning of their imminent arrival by giving a loud blast on his horn. The audible signal warned all those within earshot that any unattended children or domestic animals must be cleared from the highway. The signal alerted the passengers of the opportunity to glimpse the variety of homesteads constructed from locally sourced raw materials. Importantly, it also served to alert and make ready those who handled the mail, which was dropped and collected at regular points along the route.

It was a beautiful sunny day and the coach eventually stopped alongside a rustic roadside tavern. "Time for a break," announced the driver. "We will rest and water the horses for forty-five minutes. The inn's landlord will be pleased to see to your needs." William welcomed the break and climbed down from the coach with a feeling of relief. He realised the dust from the journey had made his throat very dry. He retrieved a carved wooden mug from his possessions and walked over to the horse trough. He raised the arm of the cast iron water pump and with a firm downward pressure, water gushed out of the spout. He looked at the water-filled mug and remembered how his father had spent many hours carving the mug by hand. For a brief moment he felt that the spirit of his father was there with him wishing him well on his journey.

"May I sit here?" William asked shyly as he approached a small group who had settled in the shade under the spreading branches of an oak tree.

The response was accompanied by warm smiles. "Of course you may," said a kindly looking elderly gentleman with a well-groomed beard. "Please make yourself comfortable." It served as a suitable haven to rest shaken limbs that had endured the rigours of the uneven surface of the main road to London, a road that was less well constructed than it had been when first laid during Roman times. William ate his lunch listening to the polite conversation of his fellow travellers while taking great pleasure in absorbing the smells, sounds and views of the surrounding rural landscape.

He greatly appreciated the temporary break from the dusty road trip, until all too soon he heard the eager tones of the driver call, "Time to move on, everybody." As the sun started to set, there appeared the profile view of a vast area of buildings on the horizon. His first glimpse of the capital city of London filled William with amazement and he felt it served as an exciting welcome to the next chapter in his life.

William thought he could detect a slight taste of sea salt on his lips as the coach finally arrived at the city terminus close by the northern bank of the River Thames. William's new master looked up at him and identified himself by holding a board with his name printed in large letters. William's first impression was one of a man with a firm but kind face and his apprehension started to wane. As he alighted from the coach the man stepped forward and enquired, "William Gascoyne I presume."

"Yes, sir," replied William politely.

The man introduced himself. "I am James Smith, master stonemason, and you will be my charge during training. Welcome to London."

After collecting the packet that contained his possessions, an excited William was directed towards a horse-drawn cart parked at the kerbside. His heightened senses were determined to absorb everything that his new environment had to offer. He was fascinated by the hustle and bustle of what seemed like an endless stream of people passing by. His attention then became distracted as he detected a not very pleasant odour that was carried by the breeze from the general direction of the river.

During their journey, William witnessed for the first time the tall masts of the sailing ships on the River Thames that carried all manner of cargo from around the world to be unloaded by lightermen into their flat bottomed boats or by stevedores at the numerous docksides. Eager to learn, William asked, "What happens to the cargo?"

With an air of confidence Mr Smith replied, "The shipped goods are taken into warehouses to await inspection by Customs and Excise officers before eventually being given clearance for distribution."

William's journey ended when the horse and cart arrived at a row of terraced houses, which formed the frontage alongside a section of canal that was linked by a set of locks to the river. The waterway served as a means to transport the raw materials by barge to the builder's yard that lay behind the row of houses. William was struck by the different architecture of these new surroundings. The yellow brick structures with flat arch window and door openings contrasted greatly with the red brick and curved brick heads to the windows back in Stony Stratford.

William was led into the end house next to the main gate to the yard. Mrs Smith welcomed him with the warmth of a mother whose own children had grown and left the family home and who now desperately desired a surrogate child to care for. The house was small but afforded adequate space for a small family. To William it was a home of comparative sophistication relative to the simple abode of The Bull yard. Pictures hung on the smooth plastered walls which were painted in an eye comforting pastel green. William placed his hand on the back of a padded chair that had been placed strategically in front of a cast iron fire grate incorporating an integral side oven. "That chair is reserved for the master of the house," advised Mrs Smith. After many years of tending a log burning fire at home, William found it fascinating to see the welcoming coal fire blazing in the grate that gave off an unfamiliar smell of coal tar. What seemed to be an oversized all-purpose pine table with four matching chairs filled a major part of the room.

Mrs Smith led William through a doorway from the front room to the scullery. "This is where I prepare the food before it is cooked on the range," she informed him. Then pointing she said, "This door to the rear leads into the builder's yard and provides access to the ashpit toilet that is shared with others in this row of houses. If you carry on beyond the toilet block you will find the yard pump that serves the needs for all the local community." On the wall adjacent to the door hung the tin bath, which was taken down once a week and placed on the floor in front of the fire. A large kettle, blackened by smoke and carbon, rested over the fire. Boiling water from the kettle together with buckets of cold water were poured into the bath and used to remove the dirt and ease the aches from physical labour.

After a much appreciated supper of soup and crusty bread, William was shown up the winding treads of the staircase that led to the landing area at first floor level which had been made over to a sleeping area for him. He undressed down to his underwear and slipped thankfully between the blankets on the straw filled mattress that lay on the bare floorboards. For the first time he heard and took notice of the new sounds that surrounded him. Despite having lived next to a drinking establishment for all of his young life, he had never registered the fact that these types of establishments emitted sounds which echoed into the late hours. Around him was the noise of raised voices and raucous laughter that informed the neighbourhood of late-night socialising that was frowned upon by polite society. These sounds at first alerted his senses to a mild form of fear and uncertainty, but gradually he was overcome by the weariness of a long and exhausting day.

CHAPTER 3

The pursuit of a wife

"Time to get up, William!" came the instruction shouted by Mr Smith from downstairs. An early start was going to be required each and every morning. William believed it was never too early in the morning to begin doing something you enjoy, and he was convinced he was going to love his new career. A bread and tea breakfast served as the first meal of the day. William and Mr Smith left the house by the back door and marched across the builder's yard to the sheds at the side of the canal wharf. Two canal barges had already tied up next to the shed. The bargee had already detached the workhorse from the harness which enabled it to haul the heavy barge load of quarry stone along the canal network whilst walking along the towpath. The cargo was piled up in the hold to the top edge of the vessel's side walls and the protective cover of tarpaulin that had protected the contents during its journey was now pulled back. Two yardmen manoeuvred a pole over the hold of the barge and were preparing a block and tackle to lift a heavy boulder onto the wagon that was waiting on the canal bank ready to transport it into the stoneyard. William followed his master into the stonemason's shed where various pieces of stone block rested at different stages of carving.

William's first day as an apprentice stonemason was one of watching, fetching and sweeping floors. He felt comfortable and happy with the trade that had been selected for him and considered that he could not have made a better choice himself. He found new friends quickly amongst the other young workers in the yard. He had great respect for the skills of the craftsmen who could take a lump of rough stone and turn it into a piece of art. He was in awe of the way the sections of stone were placed together in the workshop like pieces of a jigsaw before being dispatched to form the facade of ornate buildings along the streets of London.

William proved to be an able and willing trainee and within a relatively short time became a useful and productive investment for Mr Smith. His quick mind made him a very useful person to send out to sites to take dimensions and details for the men in the workshop to work from. He was an articulate and amiable individual who found dealing with architects and surveyors a satisfying part of a day's work. Over time the aging Mr Smith was happy to increasingly offload the burden of administration and negotiation to his young prodigy. With careful guidance the young William became an able agent to manage the existing projects and promote future business. The good name of the business often resulted in them being nominated contractors on some of the capital's most prestigious projects under the supervision of the most renowned architects. With a high reputation for quality and reliability came full order books and an increased workforce of journeymen (men who had successfully completed an official apprenticeship in a building trade or craft) were employed as the business expanded.

On Sundays William was a regular churchgoer and attended the local Anglican Church. Sunday was welcomed by the peal of bells which rang out throughout the neighbourhood. The day of rest was the opportunity for an extra few minutes in bed before putting on his best pair of trousers and a white shirt. Boots had been polished the previous evening and had been laid out ready. The status attached to the senior trade of a stonemason made it important that William should be seen and be well presented at church gatherings. The church was also the centre of the social activities which William enjoyed. At the end of the church service small groups of men would gather along the railing, which formed the boundary with the public footpath at the front of the church. Here they would gossip about the events of the previous week. Detailed accounts of incidents which had occurred were reported and commented upon and advanced notices of forthcoming events were announced. William was a gregarious person and looked forward to Sunday and the opportunity of social intercourse with a wide group, especially the young people.

The church also offered opportunity for social activities. Sunday evenings were often spent in the church hall where guest speakers gave interesting and informative accounts of their travels and experiences. Dances were arranged for the first Sunday each month and were attended by both young and old. It was at the church's midsummer dance that William first set his eyes on Martha Wills, an attractive young maidservant for a local wealthy household. She was a girl with an accent so different from William that he had to ask twice before she understood that he was inviting her to dance with him. This was both a bold and brave move by William who was not an experienced dancer and certainly not confident in making conversation with young girls.

The relationship blossomed during their regular weekly meetings as the couple engaged in lengthy conversation.

It became increasingly clear to William that he was falling deeply in love with Martha. During the annual church outing to the seaside the following spring, William finally plucked up the courage to express his feelings to her. The opportunity presented itself as the couple were enjoying the sea breeze as they strolled along the sand. William and Martha had found themselves detached from the rest of the church group and William suggested they should rest on a seafront bench until the others arrived. After a few minutes of awkward small talk William decided to make his move. "Martha," he started with a degree of apprehension in his voice, "I'm sure that you must be aware of my strong feelings for you." He cleared his throat nervously before continuing. "I hope you do not think it too forward of me to ask, but would you consider doing me the great honour of becoming my wife?" Before Martha could respond, the couple were suddenly surrounded by their follow churchgoers who had noticed them sitting on the bench.

"Well, everybody," began the group leader in a voice of undeniable authority, "it is time for us all to make our way back to the railway station to catch our train home." During William's journey home he was filled with regret that he had hesitated so long before making his approach to Martha. On their arrival back in London the group was quick to disperse and William was disappointed that he was unable to say more than a brief farewell to Martha.

William realised that waiting for another opportunity to speak with Martha alone could take some considerable time. He decided that he would write to her and make his proposal in written form. He set about composing a letter that would inform Martha of his feelings and give her an outline of his hopes and aspirations. He sat down to write with mixed feelings of excitement and hope, coupled with a fear of what the possible response might bring. He wrote:

My dear Martha

I hope you do not object to me writing to you, but my feelings for you are both genuine and honourable. I regret that I was unable to finish my proposal to you while we were alone, and I fear that it may be some time before the opportunity will come for me again. I therefore reaffirm my proposal of marriage. I hold you in the highest esteem and I would be as loyal to you as I am to Her Royal Highness our beloved Queen Victoria. It is my quest to become the best stonemason possible and to create a profitable business that would afford me a comfortable home for you and our future family. I hope you do not feel me too bold in approaching you in this manner and I await your reply with bated breath.

Your most sincere admirer and servant,
William

For William it seemed like an eternity before the next church social gathering. He had not received any response from Martha by the time he entered the busy church hall. He nervously looked around the room until he finally spied Martha, accompanied by her close friend, standing next to an open set of French doors. Much to William's consternation, it seemed that Martha's friend was reading the letter he had sent. William was filled with a concern and embarrassment that the recorded expression of his love should be shared with anyone other than its intended recipient. As William moved towards them, the girls suddenly became aware of his approach and hurriedly hid the letter and smiled shyly.

"Hello," said William unaware of what reception to expect.

"Hello," responded the two girls in chorus. It was an uncomfortable meeting initially and Martha's friend immediately announced her need to depart, using the unlikely excuse to help to make cups of tea for the assembled company.

"May we talk quietly outside?" requested William.

Martha took his arm and walked through the doorway onto a smooth flagstone patio. The air was filled with the sweet scent from the well maintained multi-coloured flower border that was now in full bloom. William guided Martha to a conveniently located ornate cast iron round table with a pair of matching chairs.

As they sat down, William spoke with a quiver in his voice. "Please don't think me forward, but I am motivated purely by good intentions and my offer of marriage is made in all sincerity." Now speaking with a little more confidence in his voice he continued, "I hope that my letter has made clear my intentions and I can quite understand your desire to seek advice from your good friend."

Martha could feel herself blush and she raised a delicate lace edged cotton handkerchief to her cheek. She had spent time embroidering it with dainty pink flowers and found its feel gave her comfort during difficult times. She spoke with much emotion in her voice. "I must confess similar feelings for you, and I am flattered by your wonderful offer, but I can't accept."

William implored her to say what he might do to make her change her mind, but her response was to dissolve into a flood of tears. William embraced her and tried to comfort her while apologising for distressing her so greatly.

Through her sobs Martha murmured, "You have no reason to be sorry, the blame for the situation is entirely mine."

"I'm sure that cannot be," William uttered in a sympathetic tone. "I beg you to tell me why you think you are to blame," he pleaded.

She finally admitted in a voice filled with guilt, "The reason I cannot marry you is because I can't read and write. I even had to get my friend to read your letter for me."

"But why should that be reason for you to feel reluctant?" William inquired.

"I would not be able to sign my name in the marriage register," Martha said with regret.

William embraced her tightly. "You do not have to sign your name," he said reassuringly. "It will not be a barrier to us getting married. I love you so much and I promise I will do anything to make you change your mind."

Martha finally gave way to her true feelings and admitted, "I love you dearly, William, and I would be proud to be your wife."

Soon after meeting for lunch, William nervously accompanied Martha to her home to seek her father's permission for their union. The Wills family had been made aware of the reason for the visit, and after formal introductions were complete William was invited to sit in a pine carver chair in front of an open fire next to Martha's father. Other members of the family provided privacy by withdrawing to a room at the back of the house. With the backing sound of crackling logs burning on the fire, William formally asked Mr Wills for permission to marry Martha. There was initial reticence shown by Mr Wills as he cross-examined William about his intentions towards his daughter. During their discussion, the realisation that the two men shared the same stonemason trade developed a rapport between them. On further investigation about William's training and career, there emerged a degree of satisfaction for Mr Wills regarding the prospects for his daughter's suitor. William felt progressively more at ease in the company of Mr Wills as their conversation continued into the afternoon. The fire started to burn down and was fed with more logs when William was eventually filled with elation as approval for the proposed union was sanctioned by Mr Wills. Martha and her mother were immediately summoned by Mr Wills so they could share in the good news. William's relief was palpable and he could not be sure whether it was his emotion or the smoke from the fire that almost brought a tear to his eye.

Although Martha was born in London her family hailed from the village of Blisworth in Northamptonshire, only ten miles from William's birthplace of Stony Stratford. The sleepy village had been woken up by the arrival of the Grand Union Canal which connected it with endless places of employment throughout the country, both north and south. The national canal system had developed during a canal building boom in the eighteenth century, when it was established that a horse hauling narrow boats and barges laden with freight could move almost fifty times more weight than a horse pulling a cart on a track. Martha's stonemason father had travelled by barge to the metropolis by working his passage. Work for his skill was in high demand in the capital and it was not long before he had established himself and was in a position to arrange for his wife to join him. The Wills family had long been settled in the capital city, but it was to the bride's ancestral village of Blisworth that the young couple travelled two months later for a church wedding ceremony on 28th February 1847 where Martha made her mark in the marriage register. Little did the young bride know how many twists and turns she would experience during her married life.

CHAPTER 4

An introduction to Royal Leamington Spa

The newly married couple spent their honeymoon during early March 1847 at the home of William's mother in the sophisticated and fashionable town of Royal Leamington Spa. His mother was now a resident in King Street in the town, where she had a regular business as a laundress. William's sister and brother still lived with their mother. Mary was employed locally as a dressmaker and James was an apprentice gilder. Although the house consisted of only two bedrooms the couple were given one of the rooms to themselves, which had been vacated voluntarily by James who slept downstairs on a sofa.

William and Martha attended the parish church of All Saints for their Sunday devotions. At conclusion of the service, an open invitation was given for the town's visitors to attend a welcome meeting held by the vicar and some local parishioners that afternoon.

"That sounds like a lovely idea," whispered Martha, and William nodded with approval. That afternoon the couple walked through the town once more to the parish church. It was a pleasant sunny day and they savoured the sweet smell emitted from the flowers that seemed to surround them everywhere. William was aware of Martha's reluctance to meet new people and he gave her hand a reassuring squeeze.

"You are truly welcome to our parish," was the greeting from the vicar standing at the main entrance to the church. As he shook hands with the couple he asked their names. William observed that the church already contained a number of visitors engaged in conversation with local residents. The vicar ushered the couple into the main body of the church towards a well-dressed couple. "This is Mr and Mrs Brown who live in nearby George Street," announced the vicar. "Please meet our visitors Mr and Mrs William Gascoyne." Martha, being unfamiliar with her relatively new title, felt a glow of pride standing next to her husband.

"So, what has attracted you to Leamington, Mr Gascoyne?" asked Mr Brown.

"We live in London but are recently married and are staying with relatives in your beautiful town," responded William.

"Oh, how wonderful!" exclaimed Mrs Brown.

"What is your business in our great capital city of London?" Mr Brown asked with intrigue.

"I am a stonemason," William replied with great satisfaction.

"What a coincidence," responded Mr Brown, "I have a building business myself with premises in Chapel Street just round the corner from my home."

"We are admiring your town," said William. "We would like to get to know it better while we are here."

"You must call on us for afternoon tea," invited Mrs Brown. "My father, Thomas Dawkes, was parish clerk of All Saints Church during the early part of this century and left an accurate account of Leamington's early growth." Mrs Brown continued modestly, "Partly in memory of my father, I have continued his work and I have become something of a local historian."

The young Gascoyne couple sat with nervous anticipation in the Browns' comfortable parlour. On a side table rested a box full of documents ready for reference during the afternoon's discourse. "It's lovely to see you again," announced Mrs Brown, entering the room with a loaded tray ready to provide tea.

"It's very kind of you to indulge us in this manner," said William.

"It's a pleasure to be able to share knowledge about the town my father loved," said Mrs Brown with more than a hint of pride in her voice as she prepared to outline her information. "I'll start by setting the scene," she said clearing her throat. "The original settlement of Leamington Priors lay on the London to Warwick turnpike road to the south of the River Leam. From its source in Northamptonshire, the River Leam wends its way through the Warwickshire countryside until it flows into the River Avon near Warwick. Leamington means 'town on the Leam' and there were two settlements of that name in Warwickshire. In order to distinguish between the two places, one became known as Leamington Priors because of its connection to the Abbey at nearby Kenilworth, while the other is referred to as Leamington Hastings in deference to the Hastings family who were the local landowners. Leamington Priors has grown from a sleepy village of three hundred inhabitants at the turn of the nineteenth century into a vibrant town of in excess of fifteen thousand people. The popularity of the local spa water resulted in the settlement becoming known as Leamington Spa and the status of the town had been greatly enhanced when granted a charter in 1838 to use the prefix 'royal' by Queen Victoria, who had stayed in the town as a young princess."

Mrs Brown paused to take a refreshing sip of her tea. "My father was born in 1767 and he witnessed first-hand the early days of the town's rapid expansion until his sad death in 1835." The couple detected a suggestion of sadness in the voice of their hostess. Mrs Brown continued. "The town owes much of its growth to local residents who recognised the commercial potential derived from the perceived health benefits of the local spa water. At the end of the eighteenth century 'taking the waters' in spa towns such as Bath and Cheltenham became fashionable, partly as a result of the disruption caused by the Napoleonic Wars which discouraged the members of the upper classes from partaking their Grand Tours of Europe. The existence of a spa water spring in the village of Leamington Priors on land controlled by the Lord of the Manor was known about for some considerable time. Lord Aylesford, a man of means and Lord of the Manor, was reluctant to allow the exploitation of the well for commercial gain. This led some members of the community to search for a source of the mineral water on land outside of Lord Aylesford's control."

Mrs Brown took another sip from her cup while emphasising that all the villagers were well known to each other. "In 1784, Benjamin Satchwell, the local postmaster, discovered a spa spring on land very close to here which is now known as Bath Street. The land belonged to his friend and local innkeeper William Abbotts and together they realised that it could be exploited for profit. Two years later they opened the first saline baths on the site. The commercial success of the 'Abbotts Saline Baths' initiated the opening of a number of bathhouses in the vicinity by others, creating much competition. Leamington followed the lead of prominent spa towns that emphasised the health benefits of mineral water. The report of a plentiful supply of spa water soon attracted fashionable people to the developing spa town to take the waters. The fact that there was a sufficient quantity of water for each client to have fresh water in their bath was a distinct advantage over other towns where the use of second-hand water was common. The drinking of the spa water was also seen as beneficial. Its use was encouraged by Dr Jephson, a local medical practitioner, who during the second and third decades of the nineteenth century became nationally renowned and included among his patients members of the royal family and the prime minister, William Gladstone."

Mrs Brown sensed that William was curious about something and enquired, "Do you have any questions so far?"

William was pleased to have the opportunity to find out more about property ownership. "Do you know who else owns land in the parish?"

"A major owner of the land is the Willes family of Newbold Comyn, although some significant parcels of land belong to the Greatheed and Wise families," replied Mrs Brown. Wanting to expand on her answer she continued. "The Willes own small pockets of land in the Leamington Priors village, but the major part of their land holding is in the Leamington Priors parish located on the northern side of the river with restricted access over a river bridge."

"How did they come by their land?" asked William full of interest.

"The Willes were a farming family originally from the nearby village of Ufton. They purchased their Leamington Priors estate during the Dissolution of the Monasteries when Henry VIII was selling off church land cheaply in order to finance his war with France."

"Are the Willes keen to sell their land for development?" asked William with added interest.

"The opportunity for the Willes family to profit from the expanding spa town during the early nineteenth century led Edward Willes to encourage residential development on his agricultural land to the north of the river. To this end he employed nationally renowned architects like John Nash to draw development plans for parcels of his land," Mrs Brown explained before taking another sip of tea.

"Even so, my father told me that there was reluctance shown by the Willes family to deal directly with developers," advised Mrs Brown. "So as to avoid dealing with speculators buying individual building plot, Willes sold large parcels of land to Joseph Vincent Barber, a landscape artist of some note from Birmingham. Barber was extremely skilful at maximising a profit from land, buying it on very favourable terms and selling it on at the most advantageous price. He divided the land he had bought into individual building plots which were sold to builders and speculators. Each plot was subject to a planning permission clause in the sale contract which controlled the size, appearance and quality of any development. In the first half of the nineteenth century, houses in Leamington with owner occupiers tended to be restricted to those who had vested interests in the town. Many other properties were placed at the disposal of visitors to the town. Having made his fortune Barber retired and travelled to Italy in 1837 but died only one year later of malaria while in Rome."

William and Martha had greatly enjoyed the hospitality and friendship shown, but reluctantly decide it was time to take their leave. They thanked their hostess for her generosity, together with her extremely interesting history of the town. Finally, William asked Mrs Brown for directions to the location of the bath houses so they might pass them on their way. They left the George Street house and walked the short distance to Bath Street before heading north past the parish church and crossing the river bridge. Their newly acquired knowledge generated an even greater interest in the buildings they passed as they walked on their journey home.

The Gascoyne family had great pleasure showing William and Martha as much as possible of their delightful spa town during the remainder of their visitors' stay. William felt that he could be happy and comfortable in this town where all the buildings were barely older than he was. Many of the terraces and crescents, with the front facades designed to look like one individual grand building, reminded him of London. He was impressed by the building elevations to the highway where stucco rendered walls embellished with pediments over openings, together with moulded pilasters crowned with Doric, Ionic or Corinthian capitals, were designed to give the appearance of carved stone. Ornate wrought ironwork used for railings and balconies painted green gave the impression that they were formed in copper that had turned from its natural brown colour due to weathering as a result of exposure to the elements. At regular intervals along the main thoroughfares lime trees gave the impression of an avenue of welcoming bystanders waving their green foliage. The majestic appearance of the town, together with the employment opportunities on offer could not fail to impress William and Martha. The farewell to the couple was accompanied with a heartfelt request from William's mother, "Please consider coming to join us living in Leamington one day."

CHAPTER 5

Early married life

The happy young married couple returned to London and rented a one-bedroom apartment in a lodging house, which was small but cosy. William's keen eye and good draughtsmanship endeared him to his employers who found his independence and reliability invaluable on building sites for which they were responsible, and where they found it difficult to devote time during their busy schedule. Despite his young age he showed great maturity and was well respected by those whose building contracts he worked on. William was soon taking on the role of the foreman mason on prestigious contracts under the supervision of the nationally famous architect Augustus Welby Pugin. His wages were good and his reputation was growing.

William's responsibilities grew even greater shortly after their return to London when Martha advised him that she had become pregnant. Their delight was tempered by the realisation that their circumstances would need to change. They agreed that their small accommodation would no longer be suitable for them to live in once the baby was born. William pondered the situation with Martha and she fully supported him in a proposal that they should move to Leamington. Their experience during their visit to the town had alerted them to the potential for a better life for them as a family. When William gave notice of his intention to leave their London base, it was met with sadness by both friends and business contacts. A leaving party was organised to wish the couple farewell and to celebrate their good news about the baby. Augustus Pugin prepared a letter of introduction and recommendation for William to present to potential new clients and architects.

During the journey to Leamington by train, their mood was sombre and it seemed to take much longer than on previous occasions. However, on arrival in Leamington they were greeted by family members and the couple's mood turned to one of great joy and elation. William and Martha moved in with his mother until the baby, a boy, was born in November 1847. The new arrival was named John in honour of William's father, much to Elizabeth's delight.

William found his family a modest cottage in Rugby Road, Lillington, a small village that was now becoming a suburb of expanding Leamington. With one room on the ground floor and one upstairs bedroom, the property was small but comfortable. The living room was entered directly from the street and was kept snug by coal burning in a cast iron range in the fireplace which also served as a means for cooking family meals. In one corner a tin bath hung on a door that gave access to a winding timber staircase to the bedroom. The toilet was housed in a brick outhouse located halfway down a long rear garden and was shared with the occupants of an adjoining property. It was an ideal starter home for a new family. It was 1847 and William was twenty-one years old. A young and ambitious William knew that it was to serve as an initial base from which they would consolidate their early family life. "One day I will build a house for our family to live in," he assured Martha, who replied with a knowing smile.

Life for the Gascoyne family was good and during the following year Martha became pregnant again. On 28th January 1849, while staying at the house of William's mother at 55 King Street, a second son, James, was born. However, the joys of January were to be overshadowed by the tragedy of May that same year. On Tuesday 15th May, young John had gone with his mother to his grandmother's house in King Street. Elizabeth Gascoyne had established a thriving laundry business at the premises since arriving in the town and Martha often called in to help her mother-in-law on busy days. She helped to keep the fire alive under the large boiling pot that was set in a brick structure in a lean-to extension at the rear of the house. The atmosphere in the room was filled with the smell of soap as fumes escaped from the cloudy bubbling water. Lines of freshly boiled sheets, shirts and other garments were strung out on the drying line in the rear garden. The hive of activity gave opportunity for John to play in the garden while James slept in a wooden cradle placed in a warm corner of the kitchen.

At around ten o'clock on this fine sunny morning John was let out to play in the garden. It was John's curiosity that made him wander out of the garden and enter a small badly constructed timber shed nearby which served as a toilet. In the ashpit privy somebody had discarded a bunch of faded flowers. It was an attempt to retrieve the flowers that encouraged John to overreach himself and fall head-first into the ashpit. It was only a short while before his mother glanced out of the small casement window and noticed that he was not in the garden. "Has anyone seen John recently?" asked Martha with obvious concern in her voice. The negative responses filled her with fear and she immediately raised the alarm.

All members of the house became engaged in a search of the surrounding area. After some frantic investigations it was agreed that the town crier should be called to make a proclamation. Neighbours were soon on the scene and the search area was extended to the neighbouring streets and properties. At around three o' clock in the afternoon two local women, Mrs Farrell and Mrs Atwood, on looking into the ashpit saw a boy's cap in the refuse and found a nearby clothes-prop to drag it out. The cap was identified by a distraught Martha as belonging to John. Another neighbour, William Whitfield, eventually discovered the dead body in the pit covered with filth and it was evident that the boy had been smothered some hours before.

Early the following morning the Gascoyne family made their way to the southern end of the town close to the cluster of public bath houses where the inquest on the boy's death was held at the town hall. They ascended the steps and entered the town hall between the four towering columns that guarded the main entrance. The strong smell of fresh polish filled the air as the family group were led by an usher through the foyer and into the coroner's courtroom. Details of the tragic event were heard in total silence apart from the sound of Martha sobbing. The coroner, Mr Greenaway, spoke in a hushed tone as he addressed the family. "I wish to express my sincere sympathy for the parents and relatives. It is clear that I have no option but to return a verdict of accidental death." He then demanded with a hint of anger in his voice, "The toilet shed which was in an unsatisfactory condition should be demolished immediately and the privy pit filled in."

The Gascoyne family followed the horse-drawn hearse carrying the child as it made its way, at a slow walking pace, down the Parade to the Leamington Priors parish church of All Saints. The funeral route was lined by groups of people at regular intervals who were keen to show their respect and support. The church contained many friends of the family and William's attention was drawn to the distinctive smell of beeswax filling the air from the large number of burning candles. William found his thoughts kept wandering to memories of his son's short life which had lasted less than two years, and for him the funeral church service and burial seemed to pass all too quickly. That night Martha told William, "I feel as though I am in a nightmare, but unlike any I have experienced before. With this one I never manage to wake up from it." Once more Martha cried herself to sleep in his arms. William knew that nothing in life could prepare a child's parent for a tragic event of this magnitude and promised himself that he would never forget his son.

William looked despairingly at his sleeping wife with a tear in his eye and whispered, "I pledge to do all I can to promote improvements in public health so that this type of tragic event will not reoccur and leave another family heartbroken."

CHAPTER 6

The impact of the railway on the development of Royal Leamington Spa

Soon after their relocation to Leamington, William began to witness significant changes in transport links to his new hometown as a result of advances in railway transport. From the early days of its modern growth, Leamington had benefited from both road and canal transport. The general poor construction and maintenance of the nation's road network rendered it unsuitable for transporting heavy and fragile goods over long distances. The high quality Bath stone that William required for his trade was hewn from distant quarries and still transported by barge along the Grand Union Canal to a local wharf. Here the boulders were offloaded from the barge with a block and tackle crane onto a horse-drawn cart for the final part of their journey. The use of heavy bulk materials delivered in this way from a remote source involved lengthy delivery dates and required William's competent planning and programming skills.

William's progressive outlook made him accepting of the potential advantages offered by modern innovations and inventions. Major improvements in rail track design, combined with significant advances in steam locomotives and rolling stock, provided a major boost for William's progress in business. The use of wagons on wooden or metal tracks had long been a method adopted for moving heavy materials. The method of ensuring that the wheels remained on the tracks was a challenge and combinations of flat wheels running in channels or on flanged rails were tried with varying degrees of success. The development of steam locomotive engines connected to wagons on flanged metal wheels running on flat rails proved to work most efficiently and made the transport of people and goods a practical, safe and economic proposition.

In 1844 the first railway terminus serving Leamington was opened at the edge of the adjoining parish of Milverton, which provided a connection to London by way of Coventry. The service proved to be such a success that the line was acquired two years later by the London and North Western Railway Company, who in the same year proceeded with plans to provide a more direct route to the capital via Rugby. In October 1852 a further line to the town was opened to the public by the Birmingham and Oxford Junction Railway which provided access for William and other residents to Birmingham as well as London.

William and the other residents of Leamington were made fully aware of the dangers that could be associated with railways. On Tuesday 11th June 1861, a fatal accident occurred on the line to Coventry on the outskirts of Leamington, when the engine and tender of a goods train fell through a bridge over the junction of four roads near Leek Wootton. An inquest held at the Kings Arms Hotel, Kenilworth, heard from local witnesses that the bridge was rumoured to be unstable. Reports from expert engineers confirmed that there were flaws in the metalwork of the structure. The jury returned confirmation that George Rowley (driver) and John Wade (fireman) were killed by the fall of engine No. 282, weighing upwards of thirty tons, through the floor of the iron girder bridge. It was agreed with the coroner that in order to allay fears in the public's mind about other local bridges, including the one at the junction of Bath Street and High Street, Leamington, that they should be inspected for safety by the London and North Western Railway Company engineers.

As a consequence of subsequent structural surveys, William was employed in 1862 by the railway company to remove the ponderous pillars in the middle of the road which had been used to support the railway bridge in High Street, Leamington, and to provide a new structure. William was granted permission by the Local Board of Health to erect two temporary supports, even though it would be necessary to stop the thoroughfare completely. The wooden portion of the old structure was almost entirely removed by William's workforce, revealing the iron bridge with tubular roofing. William carefully supervised the placing of two girders, each 154 feet in length and weighing 100 tons, spanned from wall to wall with a sufficient space for two lines of rails between them. To ensure a perfect fit, William took precise site measurements for all the girders, which were supplied by Mr Woodhall of Great Bridge, near Birmingham. He also ensured delivery of materials in strict accordance with his critical path programme for the project. On completion of the work, the general consensus was that William had executed the contract in an exemplary fashion with the minimum amount of disruption.

Competition to provide the fastest train service led the directors of the London and North Western Railway Company to issue instruction that the speed of one train daily between Birmingham to London, and vice versa, be increased to achieve a journey time of two hours. The improving speed, comfort and convenience of the transport system expanded the catchment area for potential customers in the Leamington housing market. Birmingham businessmen were drawn away from the city to the more attractive outlying dormitory towns which, with the advent of reliable railway services, had become within tolerable commuting distance. Typical of these business commuters was Gilbert Hamilton, a civil and mechanical engineer and the managing partner of James Watt and Company, formally Boulton, Watt and Company. Hamilton worked at the company's world-renowned Soho Works in Birmingham, but in the 1860s he took up residence at Leicester House, Kenilworth Road, one of the many attractive residential roads in the Leamington district.

CHAPTER 7

Seizing the opportunity for new building

A major attraction of Leamington for William and Martha was the abundance of trees and shrubs. The Improvements and Markets Bill 1843 gave the town's commissioners the power to plant trees for ornamentation, but also the right to make improvements upon land in the parish which they purchased or acquired. Many of the residential streets in Leamington were planted with a line of ornamental trees which were introduced as a means of providing employment for the poor of the town. The job creation scheme also provided the town with the benefit of creating many areas of open space which added greatly to the appearance of the town, particularly alongside the River Leam.

Land from the Willes Estate provided a prime source for William Gascoyne's house building business. William often followed an established building practice of acquiring the land and then selling the plot on to his customer with whom he entered into a contract to build the house. William had calculated that this particular type of transaction helped keep his borrowing to a minimum, gave him a manageable business cashflow and substantially reduced the financial risk in the overall deal. He studied the local housing market and was aware that the early development of Leamington was seen by people with wealth as an opportunity to invest in property which could accrue in value at a greater rate than the returns they could achieve on the stock market.

Builders and building companies had risen and failed from speculative building ventures that had made Leamington the shining example of a fashionable town that responded to the pleasures of the rich and famous. The return to Leamington was William's opportunity to establish himself as a master craftsman. It was a time when the construction industry in the town was in a state of revival. Cycles of building booms and slumps, which were prevalent during Leamington's growth in the early nineteenth century, culminated in a collapse of the property market as a consequence of the failure of Leamington Bank in 1837, only two years after it had been established. This event led directly or indirectly to the bankruptcy of many people, including thirty of the largest builders in the town between 1837 and 1841. This left a void in the local building industry which could be filled by new entrants to the market, like William Gascoyne, whose unblemished reputation allowed them to take advantage of the situation when the eventual recovery took place. It was a challenging environment which stimulated and excited William. Things were starting to go well with his work and his cashflow and his bank balance was starting to impress his bank manager.

The depression in the market for development land in the period prior to the 1850s had provided the wealthier members of the community with a wider choice of location for building, together with the opportunity to build detached villas in large plots at relatively economic cost. The widespread nature of the town's growth was further encouraged by the Improvement and Market Act of 1843 which promoted development around the perimeter of Leamington Priors' parish boundary in the suburb of Milverton. The provision of the bill allowed the

Leamington Town commissioners to culvert the brook which formed the boundary between the two parishes and allowed them to make improvements on land in the adjoining parish which they might purchase or acquire. By these provisions the roads and ways on the Milverton side of the brook were laid out for building speculators, a fact which led to much criticism, for it was maintained that each house that was built at Milverton took a family away from Leamington.

By this time terraces had gone out of fashion for the best houses. Now the more expensive type of houses being built were large detached or semi-detached buildings. William recognised the potential in the housing market was for the provision of substantial properties which were being purchased by the emerging middle class with newly acquired wealth created from industry and commerce.

William realised that with improving transport links, Leamington was becoming more accessible for people with business interests in other larger urban and industrial centres, who wished to establish their family home in the more pleasant environment of a spa town. The imposing residence of Thorn Bank, built during the late 1850s, provided an early opportunity for William to produce an example of the high quality craftsmanship his company could produce. Set in substantial grounds on the Warwick New Road at a convenient distance from the town's first railway station of Milverton, the large house was ornately finished with fine examples of Rococo decorative plasterwork, stained glass windows and stone fire surrounds. The extensive grounds later provided a perfect environment for Sam Lockhart, the world-renowned elephant trainer, to exercise his Ceylon elephants "The

Three Graces". Sam was born in Leamington in 1851, the second child of a circus family. When in 1871 a permanent circus was established in The Colonnade along the bank of the River Leam, Sam and his elephants became a familiar sight around the town. A popular spectacle for residents was watching the elephants bathing in the river, which they accessed via specially constructed slipways.

William was conscious that the rapid development of the town also demanded the provision of less expensive accommodation for those required to build and service the new homes of the wealthy middle class. There was a steady influx of journeymen and labourers involved in construction, and by the middle of the nineteenth century domestic servants made up almost twenty per cent of the town's population. Attached, flat fronted properties were a common street layout for cheaper housing, although changes in government taxation affecting the building industry were evident in the changing trends in their design. The incorporation of a bay window incurred the use of additional building materials, some of which were subject to a tax. However, the burden on the house owner through both direct and indirect taxation for incorporating a bay window was removed over a relatively short period when taxes on glass and bricks were abolished in 1845 and 1850 respectively.

The burden of income tax at that time was seven pence in the pound and was considered excessive by a significant body of people. An attempt by Chancellor of the Exchequer, Sir Charles Wood, to impose a new tax on houses in place of the Window Tax was defeated by a coalition of his own supporters, and his opposition indicated how sensitive taxes directed at the householder had become. Consequently, rows of flat fronted terraced houses soon became superseded by terraced houses incorporating a bay window which allowed a better outlook onto the street for the occupants. William was quick to take advantage of the changes and introduced bay windows as a feature in a development of twenty-three terraced houses he built for sale in Villiers Street, Leamington.

A drive towards the greater use of windows and glazing in buildings was taken to a new level when Prince Albert became the most high-profile personality associated with the Great Exhibition in 1851. The exhibition, a showcase of products from home and abroad, was available to the many visitors who journeyed to see it from all parts of the country and overseas. Housed in a glazed cast iron structure in Hyde Park and designed by Joseph Paxton, it acquired the nickname the "Crystal Palace" when referred to as such in an article by the English playwright Douglas Jerrold in *Punch* magazine.

William like many other local people was encouraged to attend the show by a report headed "The World's Marvels in the Crystal Palace" which appeared in the *Leamington Courier* on 10th May 1851. The introduction of cheap excursions by the railway companies from various parts of the country, including Leamington, helped to make the journey affordable to many and contributed to its success. Thomas Cook, who had established his business some ten years earlier, took advantage of the opportunity to expand his travel company by offering organised outings by train to the exhibition which eventually achieved visitor numbers in the region of six million, approximately one third of the country's total population. The exhibition lasted for five months and the adventure was further encouraged by London traders, such as E. Moses and Sons, who placed advertisements in the local Leamington press to encourage visiting parties whilst in the capital to attend their establishment. Elias Moses and Sons was a firm of tailors that recognised a growing demand for affordable fashionable clothing. They successfully introduced new methods of manufacture and marketing based on high turnover and small profit margins. By 1850 they had become a prominent tailor in London with numerous shop outlets that provided mass-marketing of men's clothing.

The exhibition provided William and other builders with a greater awareness of the materials and equipment available to them and served as a stimulus to architects and consumers. The domestic construction industry during the nineteenth century experienced a period of unprecedented activity in building of all types. The Great Exhibition provided manufacturers with the opportunity to promote their companies and showcase their new and innovative products. George Jennings, a sanitary engineer and plumber, took the opportunity to create the first public flush toilets when he installed his Monkey Closets in the exhibition's retiring rooms. During the exhibition over three quarter of a million visitors paid one penny each to use this facility and as a result the phrase "to spend a penny" was established as a common euphemism for going to the toilet. The structure of the Crystal Palace exhibition hall itself served as a prime example of how standardisation and prefabrication could assist in improving the speed of construction. This not only benefited the home market. The export of prefabricated buildings produced in Britain and shipped to parts of the Empire, as far away as Australia, offered instant accommodation for settlers.

The building industry remained largely labour intensive, but output was increasingly assisted by the introduction of mechanical devices which increased production and often improved quality. The interest of William, together with other stonemasons, was stimulated by a review about the William's Patent Stone Cutting Machine, which operated with chisels inserted in a revolving drum that could smooth the surface of granite, limestone or sandstone equal to that accomplished by the human hand. Although William was an advocate of innovation and modern materials, he was cautious about the introduction of machinery. He knew from experience that the introduction of machines did not always result in reducing overall cost, as the savings they produced were often countered by significant increases in labour costs and a reduction in labour output.

CHAPTER 8

Public health matters

William's work made him very familiar with the comfortable accommodation enjoyed by the wealthier members in society, but he was also very aware of properties occupied by the less fortunate residents of the town. Many poor people lived in small dwellings in back streets or courts, often with contiguous boundaries to the properties of the rich. William knew that many of the homes were cheaply and badly built and very quickly became slums. He made no secret of his aim to improve the building and living conditions for all the residents of the town. In order to witness the public health conditions in one of the poorest living areas, William approached one of his employees, Henry Whitehead, to arrange to visit the court where he lived. William regarded Henry as an intelligent, reliable and gentle person for whom he had developed a great respect, who through no fault of his own had fallen on hard times.

As William walked down Satchwell Street he could see Henry standing at the corner of a building under a dimly lit gas lantern perched on a cast iron lamp post at the entrance to the court where he lived. As he stretched out his hand to greet him, William's voice travelled down the narrow passageway that was just wide enough to allow a handcart to pass through. "Good evening, Henry, thank you for allowing me to visit you."

"You're welcome, sir, it's good to know that a person of your standing is interested and concerned about the place where we live." The pair walked along the flagstone and blue brick paved passage as they were dodged by a large number of excited children running around them playing a game of chase.

As they toured the court, William was eager to record as many facts as possible in support of his mission to promote improvements. William was struck by the loud volume of the constant cacophony emanating from the closely packed buildings of the court. He cleared his throat and asked his first question. "Where do get your fresh water from for the properties?"

"We all rely on a public water pump in the courtyard."

As they walked to the far end of the court, William became increasingly aware of the pungent smell in the courtyard and he instinctively took a handkerchief from his pocket and raised it to his nose. "And what provision is made for toilets?"

"This is our row of four cubicles at the end of the building. Each of the privies is shared by several families. I would let you inspect them but I'm sorry to say they are not very pleasant."

William ventured forward towards one of the cubicles before deciding to retreat. "Are there regular collections to empty the contents of the buckets?"

"There are, but there is a common practice of emptying privy buckets in the street at the time when they are to be cleared by the 'night-men' with their cart. You may imagine how objectionable this is." There was now a hint of embarrassment in Henry's voice.

In an effort to ease the situation, William changed the direction of his enquiries. "How suitable is the accommodation for the people living here?"

"Overcrowding is commonplace with as many as nine people living in the same house that has only one eight-foot square sleeping room," said Henry as he moved away and spoke to a man and his wife who were standing in the doorway of one of the dwellings. On his return he informed William that they had been given permission to look inside the couple's rented room if he wished. William viewed the room which contained very few possessions and no recognisable bed; it was evident that the occupants used the floor as the resting place for their tired bodies. William was not impressed by what he had seen, but not surprised. He was conscious that there existed a number of other significant public health issues in the town. He was aware that there were about eight hundred pigsties at private houses in the town, and a total of nineteen slaughterhouses were located in Warwick Street and Regent Street, two of the main roads in the new town area.

William understood that poor standards in public health were exacerbated by the industrial development and urbanisation of the nineteenth century. Whenever possible he argued that, "the situation presented a pressing need for some form of statutory control over buildings." William gave his support to an emerging movement directed towards the establishment of a National Building Act. Between 1845 and 1847, a series of "Model Acts" were passed which were deemed to be suitable for inclusion in the Town Improvements Clauses Act of 1847.

Pressure for even greater health controls was stimulated by a National Cholera epidemic in 1848 and the Public Health Act of the same year established a standard for the operation and responsibility of local authorities in the field of public health. The act required that plans be deposited for streets, drainage and buildings before work commenced. Local Boards of Health were created and were responsible for compiling laws for their respective towns, which were no longer required to be sanctioned by parliament, but by the newly established National Board of Health.

Despite the opposition shown by some, public health was regarded with paramount importance for the town of Leamington, which was portrayed nationally as a place for healthy living. Mr George Clark, who conducted a public enquiry on behalf of the General Board of Health, stated that Leamington, "could not afford even to be a very healthy town, it had to be superlatively healthy." William had a profound belief that the maintenance of good public health depended on transparency and the early sharing of information. When *The Times* in January 1849 wrongly announced that cholera had broken out in Leamington, the town commissioners were quick to demand a denial. However, when cholera did eventually break out in September of the same year, there was reluctance on the part of leading members of the town to publicise the fact.

William welcomed Leamington's adoption of the Public Health Act in 1850 but expressed concern when it became the subject of a protracted debate, mainly due to antagonism from certain parties with vested interests, whose political influence, land ownership, or financial position might be affected. Particular resistance came from the existing oligarchy of the town's Improvement Commissioners, together with local large estate owners Charles Bertie Percy of Guys Cliff House and the Earl of Warwick.

The concern about maintaining the good health of the town's inhabitants was the stimulus for providing and improving the means of treating and disposing of the town's sewage. In a proactive move, William established a civil engineering section within his company capable of undertaking major drainage projects in the town. The first sewage pipes in the town had been laid in 1838 but discharged into and polluted the River Leam. In 1856 the decision was taken to provide a sewage scheme on land by the river near the railway viaduct. A contract was awarded for large drainage pipes to be laid during 1862 to convey waste to the sewage works where it was treated with lime.

CHAPTER 9

Building a family home

Two years after the tragic event which led to the death of their first child, William and Martha became proud parents once again. On 24th August 1851 a son named William was born, whom they baptised in Lillington parish church. This was followed by the birth of their first daughter Elizabeth on 27th February 1854. Born in their grandmother's house in King Street, these joyful events to some degree helped to heal the mental wounds created by the tragedy of John's death that had previously devastated the inhabitants at this address.

The motivation to provide for his expanding family encouraged William to focus on his natural building skills and make a concerted effort to develop and expand his business interests. He called upon his former links with architect Augustus Welby Pugin to provide introductions to potential clients and help deliver success in obtaining more building work. This he achieved with increasing success and a greatly enhanced reputation. The opportunity to employ William's talents on projects was fortuitous for the fledging architectural practice of Edward Welby Pugin and James Murray. Murray was a native of Ireland and had served his indenture with a Liverpool based architect before moving to Coventry. He entered into partnership in the Midlands with Edward Welby Pugin, the son of Augustus, before they relocated to London in 1856 where they established a successful practice.

In 1855 William was awarded a contract by the Warwick Corn Exchange Company for the erecting of a Corn Exchange according to the plans and specification of James Murray on the site of the Castle Hotel in the Market Place, Warwick. The substantial rendered brick structure was entered via an ornate doorway flanked on both sides by arched windows. The frontage was crowned with a large circular clock in a raised decorative parapet surround. The contract was completed on time and to the good quality standard of finish expected for a public building of this type, particularly in a prominent position in the centre of the county town. The exchange proved to be a success and the Warwick Corn Exchange Company indicated its satisfaction during the following year by awarding William's company a contract in the sum of £1,210 for the enlargement of the Corn Exchange building.

During 1857 William undertook the construction of a new town hall and markets in Rugby, again under the supervision of Coventry architect James Murray and the firm of Pugin and Murray, London. The design had been selected by competition. The site of Rugby's first town hall was in place of the Elborowe School and alms houses and the foundation stone was laid on 22nd June 1857. The ground floor of the building comprised committee rooms for the use of County Court Mechanics' Institute, a library and newsroom. From an imposing front entrance a stone staircase led up to the upper floor which formed an impressive assembly hall 75 feet long by 32 feet wide. Behind the main building was attached the Corn Exchange together with a covered market for greengrocers, butter, milk and poultry dealers, which was accessed by a back street. The building was built entirely of bricks with dressings and moulded work in Bath stone. The whole project was completed by William's company in seven months at a cost of £3,170. The opening of the building on Tuesday 6ᵗʰ April 1858 was celebrated by a public dinner which William attended along with more than two hundred of the town's inhabitants.

William was increasingly gaining in confidence and reputation. He was prepared to undertake contracts that were much more remote from Leamington. His early experience of working in the metropolis gave him confidence in 1857 to build a new school for St. Peter's Roman Catholic Church in Woolwich, London. This was another Pugin and Murray project designed by the twenty-one year old Edward Webley Pugin. St. Peter's Church had been established as a place of worship for Irish soldiers who were stationed at Woolwich garrison. The initial architectural work for the parish had been undertaken by Edward's now deceased father, Augustus Webley Pugin, a renowned advocate of the Gothic Revival style. Although the Pugin and Murray practice had recently relocated to London, Edward was still based in Birmingham. He was fully aware that his regular attendance at the site would be difficult and he was confident that he could reliably delegate the day to day supervision to William. The involvement of a young and relatively inexperienced architect raised concern from the incumbent parish priest, while the awarding of the contract for £1,736 to a builder from the provinces resulted in a degree of discontent from unsuccessful tenderers. The working combination of the architect and the builder proved a good choice, and the project was successfully completed by the end of 1858 to the satisfaction of the bishop's representative and was regarded as value for money.

With the intention of providing a better home for his family, together with better facilities for his business activities, William in early 1855 made the decision to purchase a sizable parcel of land in Leamington with double frontage to Newbold Road and Cross Street. The property was sandwiched between substantial houses on both sides and provided sufficient space for a house and extensive workshops. The bold purchase of the site put great strains of William's finances and it seemed for a while that poor cashflow and a late payment to the Local Board of Health for general district rates of 1 shilling $8^{1}/_{2}$ pence might bring an early end to his enterprise. However, the successful completion of his contracts, and the punctual settlement of his accounts by his clients, allowed William to settle with his creditors and apply for venture capital.

The Gascoyne company workshop was a temporary structure to begin with, but as lucrative contracts came to completion William had by 1860 created substantial and extensive structures for his workforce which stretched along Cross Street. In the workshop large blocks of Bath stone were worked by skilled stonemasons to adorn ecclesiastic and public buildings as well as the houses for some of the wealthier members of English society. William's advanced stonemason skills were employed to supervise the marks made on the setting out floor as templates for stone cutting. William paid great attention to quality control and ensured that work was always completed to the highest standard. He ensured that a trade foreman was employed to supervise each of the Gascoyne workshops and an experienced site manager was responsible for each of the company's building sites.

William's early relation with his workforce was one of mutual respect and he showed a paternal interest for his employees. He generously shared some of the rewards gained from the success of his company. Every December the Gascoyne workshops were cleaned and decorated for the annual custom of entertaining his men on Christmas Eve. By Christmas 1860 it was usual for upwards of seventy of his men to be provided with a meal of good old English fare, followed by ample quantities of ale. William added to the joyful atmosphere of the occasion by providing music from the local saxhorn band of Messrs Wells, Hall, Weeks and Lovell. The entertainment continued until midnight, when everybody departed well pleased. The *Leamington Courier* considered it to be a significant event in the community and of interest to its readers. It was able to report that, "A thoroughly good feeling exists between Mr Gascoyne and those employed by him".

In order to further cement the business relationship with James Murray, William instructed him to design a suitable four-storey family home for his ever-expanding family. On 6th November 1855, approval was sought for a house on William's land in Newbold Road. The front of the house had a classical facade rather than the Gothic style favoured by Pugin which was the vogue for many at this time. William used the opportunity to demonstrate his stonemason skills to potential local clients by using an ashlar Bath stone front. This type of facade was novel in the town due to limited availability of suitable local building stone, together with the greater labour cost of building with stone. As a symbol of his pride in his home and country, William required that the design incorporate a pair of carved stone lions above the front entrance.

Leamington had predominantly relied on building homes with bricks produced by a local company based at the nearby clay pit. However, Leamington's development as a spa town had modelled itself on the grand spa town of Bath. In order to mimic the appearance of the stone building facades in that fine city, the brick frontage of the terraces and crescents in Leamington were covered with a sandstone coloured render to imitate Bath stone. To enhance the appearance, lines were struck in the render to suggest construction joints between blocks of stone. It later became popular to paint the rendered front of these buildings.

The new Gascoyne family house was nearing completion when William and Martha had a second daughter, Ann. She was born on 15th January 1856 and once again the birth took place at William's mother's house in King Street. By the end of June the house had been completed to a point at which the family could take occupation. On 27th September 1856 William published a "Notice of Removal" in the local press which gave thanks for patronage during the past four years and advising that his residence was now No.1 Newbold Road, Leamington, and access to his office and building yard was in Cross Street.

Martha was delighted with the home created by her husband. "You have made me the most fortunate and happiest woman in Leamington," she declared as William escorted her through the front door on their first day of occupation. The size of the Gascoyne family continued to grow during the subsequent years with the addition of daughters Martha on 28th August 1857 and Emily on 28th May 1859. Their youngest son Gustavus arrived on 24th April 1861, and their final child Juliet on 27th January

1864. These last four children were all born in the family house that William had built. The property afforded William a comfortable home for his wife and children while offering him the opportunity to maximise his involvement with the activities in his workshop when he was not overseeing work on his building sites.

The footprint of the new Gascoyne home was typical of the period. Three stone steps led up to a half glazed front entrance door which opened into a bright entrance hall. A patterned floor created with a mixture of coloured glazed clay tiles lead to a stone staircase with an oak handrail on ornate iron spindles. On the right-hand side of the hall were two rooms that were entered through timber moulded panelled doors. The front reception room contained a bay window which afforded the occupants an excellent view in both directions of the street outside. The rear room was a dining room with a large south facing window which attracted the early morning sunlight. Built-in cupboards were fitted on either side of the chimney breast. Each room had an ornate plaster ceiling cornice and ceiling rose. Both also contained a finely carved timber fire surround with a tiled cast iron insert and tiled hearth. From the hall a set of blue brick steps provided direct access to the rear garden.

To the front of the house at first-floor level there was a spacious drawing room that extended across the full width of the house. During the daytime the room was filled with light through two large sash windows which provided a pleasant view of the majestic curved row of houses that formed Lansdowne Crescent opposite. A mahogany fire surround with a mirror overmantel formed a focal point at the far end of the room. The walls and ornate ceiling were painted in pastel colours that provided a calm and soothing atmosphere for the family to relax together. The remainder of the first floor together with the second floor provided family bedrooms.

A panelled timber spandrel with a matching door provided access from the hall down steps to the basement. The basement area of the house was partly set below ground level and provided the servants' accommodation. The largest room in this area was the kitchen where all the meals for the household were prepared. The food was cooked on a large coal-fired range that was set into the chimney breast alcove. Next to the kitchen was a cold room where meats were hung on hooks from the ceiling and other foods were stored on wooden shelves or cold stone slabs. Other offices included the scullery and a wine store. The entire basement had a hardwearing floor of flagstones. Windows set into lightwells provided ventilation and natural light. To maximise the light level as much as possible, the walls were flush pointed brickwork painted white. The servants were summoned by bells fixed on a board over the dining room doorway in the hall. The bells were operated by a series of pull wires running to call points in the various rooms of the house.

CHAPTER 10

The developing support network for the construction industry

Support trades and supply services became increasingly important for those operating in the construction industry. The chisels used by the stonemasons in Gascoyne's workshop were kept sharp by the local blacksmith, conveniently located in his yard in Swan Street on the opposite side of Newbold Road. As was his custom, William issued a strict instruction to George, the current senior stonemason apprentice: "I am delegating responsibility to you for overseeing that good chisels are available to each mason. You must ensure that sharp tools are maintained at all times for producing the high quality carving expected from this company." George had a good relationship with Mr Ward the blacksmith and often assisted with the sharpening process by braving the intense heat from the incandescent charcoal to place the blunt chisels in the forge, the atmosphere filled with fumes from scorching metal as Mr Ward removed the glowing iron from the furnace with a pair of tongs. He forged it into shape on his anvil with loud blows from a heavy hammer. Once sharpened the chisels were cooled and hardened by dipping them in a bucket of cold water that reacted by bubbling and releasing a cloud of steam. Mr Ward's duties also included that of farrier for shoeing horses belonging to the Gascoyne company. When not working for William, the blacksmith's bellows and furnace were rarely idle trying to satisfy the demand for bespoke decorative wrought ironwork which adorned so many of the town's buildings.

William obtained a constant supply of timber from local sawmills for use by his carpenters and joiners. The sawmill owner was responsible for supplying suitable timber that was sorted and graded appropriate to its eventual use. Gascoyne's yard echoed to the clatter of timber planks being offloaded from a delivery wagon. William's joinery foreman, with clipboard in hand, inspected each length of timber to ensure the quantity and quality matched the order placed. Once checked as all correct, he stored his pencil in the pocket of his tweed jacket and turned to the men with him: "You are to stack each length of timber on the correct shelf in the storage rack, and as you do it you must ensure that there is a suitable gap around each piece of the seasoned wood to allow a free flow of fresh air to circulate." Each shelf was arranged to allow the various pieces to be neatly stacked for ease of identification and access. Seasoned construction timber was sawn to finished size ready for use as floor joists and structural roof members. Good quality timber with few knots was taken into the machine shop to be planed and moulded for architrave, skirting or dado rail. The best quality timber was allocated for use in the carpentry workshop to produce joinery components such as windows and doors.

The ability for trade suppliers to carry stock and extend credit to William and other builders was a significant factor in the eventual format of companies operating in a modern construction industry. Credit extended by the financial institutions provided opportunity for suppliers to offer monthly trading accounts to support building contractors like William. By the mid-nineteenth century the supply of building materials and equipment was increasingly provided by merchants who stocked a wide range of items and acted as intermediaries between the primary producers and the building companies.

William obtained his materials from various local builder's merchants. George Nelson, who conducted his business from Edmondscote Mills on the outskirts of Leamington, provided a wide range of heavy goods to local builders including timber, slates, bricks, drainpipes, stone, slabs, cement and plaster. For decorative items, William used the services of William Holland at Coten End, Warwick, whose range of goods included decorative glass, wood carving, wallpapers from both British and foreign manufacturers and ornate plumbing and sanitary ware. Many products available from Holland's company had received awards for their quality at the Great Exhibition of 1851.

The financing of building projects in Leamington had initially been provided through private funding by the landowner or developer, often with the financial support of friends by private agreement, or lenders provided by solicitors who acted as intermediaries. As financial institutions developed, the system became more sophisticated. Despite the damage caused by the demise of the Leamington Bank in 1837, banks generally retained an important function as an intermediary between those like William requiring funds for building work and those with money available for investment. The establishment of Joint Stock Banks and their protection under Limited Liability Acts in 1858 and 1862, together with the trend for banks to amalgamate into a more sophisticated regional or national network of branch banking, combined to give the banking system an element of greater financial security.

The system of banks receiving deposits from those with surplus funds to be lent to entrepreneurs such as William, with the intention of achieving a profit from interest over an agreed repayment period, became a common practice. In January 1850, the Leamington Priors and Warwickshire Banking Company advertised the fact that it had received frequent applications to accept small deposits at interest. In response the bank was adopting the system pursued by the Scottish and Irish Joint Stock Banks of receiving deposits of £1 and upwards, allowing interest thereon at a rate of three per cent per annum. Deposits could be withdrawn at seven days' notice, but no interest was paid if withdrawn in less than three months.

In 1856, the Leamington Priors and Warwickshire Bank purchased the Bedford Hotel at a cost of £4,400. Mr Bateman, the bank's architect, was called in to inspect the site and to prepare plans for the conversion of the building to accommodate a new banking hall and offices. His plans were approved by the bank's directors on 9th October, and he was asked to advertise for tenders for the contract. On 12th November 1856 the directors considered eight tenders and William Gascoyne was awarded the contract on the basis of his tender for £2,475, less £230 for old materials and other adjustments. The property was substantially rebuilt including the whole front elevation. The premises were opened to the public on Monday 26th October 1857 and the directors reported at a shareholders' meeting on 15th January 1858 that the full transfer to the new premises had been completed. The bank recorded that the final price exceeded the original contract figure, but despite this William had successfully completed the work to the client's total satisfaction and he was employed for further work to that building and on the neighbouring buildings.

As the project progressed, William was intrigued to hear from his foreman about the history of the building. "The first twenty houses built in the new town area were located in a terrace on the junction of Regent Street and running southward along the west side of the Parade. In order to take advantage of the growing demand by visitors for overnight accommodation in the town, a section of the terrace was purchased and opened as the Bedford Hotel. The hotel came to prominence as a popular meeting place for a group of young men including a wealthy extrovert called John Mytton, squire of Halston in Shropshire." The foreman stopped to enquire, "Have you heard about Mytton?"

"No," replied William, who was now keen to know more about him.

"Well," said the foreman pleased to share his local knowledge, "in 1826, after a day riding with the Warwickshire Hunt, Mytton and a group of friends enjoyed a meal in the first-floor dining room of the Bedford. Following their usual practice of consuming large quantities of wine, Mytton bragged that his horse 'Mad Tom' was by far the best hunter in the county and that he would take on any wager to prove it. A challenge was made that he should use his horse to jump from the dining room onto the road below." William became engrossed as the foreman continued to tell his story. "Apparently Mytton was never one to flinch from a challenge and he left the room. He soon astounded members of the party by riding his horse up the staircase leading to the room and jumping over the dining table."

"Did he leap through the window on his horse?" asked William now gripped with suspense.

"No," replied the foreman as his tone became more serious. "Alarmed that he intended to fulfil the life-

threatening stunt, the group eventually dissuaded Mytton."
The wayward antics of Mytton and his associates met with
the general disapproval from the more upright members of
Leamington society who wished to maintain the dignity of
the town. The infamous event was widely reported and
there was a degree of satisfaction expressed by many
Leamington residents when the hotel was eventually
closed and the building sold.

The front facade of the Leamington Priors and
Warwickshire Bank, with its smooth-faced stone
decorated with ornate stone carved detailing, provided the
opportunity for William to demonstrate his skill as a
stonemason in the most prominent location in the town.
He was so proud of his completed work he took the
opportunity early one morning, before the shop traders
opened for business, to have his photograph taken in front
of the building in a traffic-free Parade. Stone buildings in
Leamington, with very few exceptions, became the work
of William Gascoyne's company. These prestige
buildings had access to substantial budgets which allowed
the use of expensive non-local stone suitable for building
purposes, together with the services of highly skilled
stonemasons.

CHAPTER 11

A devoted royalist enjoys Queen Victoria's visit to Royal Leamington Spa

William, like his parents, was a patriot and a devoted royalist. Whenever possible during his time in London he took the opportunity to witness royal processions through the city. During 1857, the first rumours of a likely visit by the monarch to Leamington filled William with excited anticipation. He enthusiastically shared the good news with the other members of his family. "This will be such a prestigious event and a great honour for our town. We must make every effort to make it a grand occasion for all to enjoy."

It was to be the first time that Queen Victoria paid a return visit to the spa town since she had come as a young princess in 1830. At that time she was travelling across the centre of England on her way to Malvern with her mother the Duchess of Kent and Sir John Conroy, who was rumoured to be the duchess's lover. The party stayed at the Regent Hotel on the main street of the town and the stop was greatly enjoyed by the young princess. The hotel had been opened by Mr Williams in 1819, the year of Victoria's birth, and lay claim to be the largest hotel in Europe consisting of one hundred bedrooms, but only one bathroom. It was initially named the Williams Hotel, but it was renamed in September later that year after a stay by the Prince of Wales, the future King George IV. Victoria turned eighteen years of age on 24th May 1837 and became Queen during the following month on the death of her uncle, William IV. Her coronation took place on 28th

June 1838 at Westminster Abbey. An indication of the fond memories she held from her brief association with the town was shown in the same year when she was successfully lobbied for Leamington Spa to use the word "royal" as a prefix.

Initially Victoria was a popular monarch, but her reputation soon suffered as events at court tarnished her reputation. Her mother's lady-in-waiting, Lady Flora Hastings, was alleged to have had an affair with Sir John Conroy. Sometime in 1839, Lady Flora developed an abdominal growth that was widely rumoured to be a pregnancy and this seemed to be confirmed when she refused an examination by the Queen's physician, Sir James Clark. Victoria suspected Conroy to be the father of the child. When Lady Flora finally agreed to an examination by the royal doctors, the accusation about the pregnancy proved to be false and it was discovered that she had an advanced cancerous liver tumour. Lady Flora died soon after in London on 5th July 1839, but her brother and Conroy made public their feelings about the unfair treatment Lady Flora had received.

Unfortunately for Victoria, another event occurred around the same time which became known as the "Bedchamber Crisis". Lord Melbourne declared his intention to resign as prime minister when his support in parliament was waning and his ability to pass legislation was becoming difficult. The Duke of Wellington declined Victoria's request to become prime minister and she reluctantly turned to Robert Peel to form a Tory administration. Peel accepted the invitation on the condition that Queen Victoria replaced some of her ladies of the bedchamber, who were wives of Whig politicians with the wives of members from his own party. Victoria regarded the ladies as close friends and confidantes, and Peel's proposal was a condition to which she could not agree. Peel refused to form the new government and Melbourne was eventually persuaded by Victoria to remain as prime minister. These political uncertainties further added to people's concerns about the Queen's ability to provide stability. Despite the bad publicity, young William continually took a supportive view of the head of state throughout these events. "Our dear Queen is above these sordid events," he asserted, "and I will always be a true and loyal servant."

The popularity of the monarch was restored by a series of events during the following year. First of these was when Victoria married Prince Albert of Saxe-Coburg and Gotha on 10th February 1840. Soon after the marriage, the mood of the country was further lifted when it was announced that Victoria was pregnant. It was in June of the same year that the first of a number of attempts to assassinate the Queen occurred during her reign. On her way by open carriage with Albert to visit her mother, a man called Edward Oxford fired shots at her at Constitution Hill, close to Buckingham Palace. Oxford was apprehended and later tried for high treason but found not guilty on grounds of insanity and committed to a lunatic asylum. This outrage against the pregnant queen, together with the birth of her baby girl Victoria on 21st November 1840, served to boost her popularity.

During 1857 Queen Victoria gave birth to the last of her nine children and when it became known that she, together with her husband, was to visit Leamington the following year, there was an air of great excitement around the town. It was announced that Lord Leigh of nearby Stoneleigh Abbey, the Lord Lieutenant of the

County of Warwickshire, would on 16th June escort the royal couple from the Kenilworth Road in the north of the town along the main street of the town to the road in the south leading to Warwick Castle. Keen to present his royalist credentials, William submitted a letter to a meeting of the Leamington Board of Health on 1st June 1858, offering to contribute £10 to the fund connected with the Queen's visit, and requesting the privilege of erecting a viewing platform at the prominent location on the Parade in front of Denby Villa adjacent to the Regent Hotel. Both the Villa and the hotel were owned by Mr Lyas Bishop, a prominent resident of the town who came originally from Hedon, Yorkshire. On acceptance of his offer, William instructed his men to set about creating the temporary structure. The sound of sawing and hammering rang out across the Parade as the platform took shape. Similar construction sounds were repeated along the full length of the proposed royal route as other builders also made preparation.

On the day of the royal visit William was at his workshop early together with his employees. He elevated himself on a suitable block of stone to address his workforce. "As you are aware today's visit is a proud moment in the history of our town. To mark this occasion and to allow you to appreciate the event, you have been given a holiday. In addition, it is my intention to give each of you sufficient money to buy refreshments from the street vendors." The offer was greeted with a rousing cheer from his men. After collecting their money, each made his way to join others enjoying the day in the town.

On a sunny Wednesday morning at 11am, spectators started to take their places along the route of the royal procession which had been decorated with flags and bunting. From his earliest days in business, William believed that first impressions were important and always took pride in his appearance. When meeting clients he always made an imposing figure in a charcoal grey three-piece suit and a top hat. "How do I look?" he asked Martha as he entered the drawing room in his best three-piece suit with his father's gold watch and chain hanging from the pocket of his waistcoat.

"You look very dapper and will not fail to impress Her Majesty." William had a spring in his step as he led the way for members of his family household to claim a prominent viewpoint at the edge of his recently constructed grandstand. William's mother and sister joined the group in order to provide child support for Martha who needed to breastfeed her two month old daughter and namesake Martha. As the group made their way slowly along Holly Walk towards the Parade, they were surrounded by a buzz of excitement as people everywhere seemed to be waving flags. William organised comfortable seats for his party on the grandstand and arranged for staff from the nearby Regent Hotel to provide them with refreshments. Before going on a tour to inspect the town's preparations, he leaned over the wicker cradle containing baby Martha and gave her a loving peck on the forehead.

Barely able to contain his excitement William left saying, "I will see you here when Her Majesty passes by."

As William strolled northwards along the main road, he was filled with pride by how well the town's people had presented such a clean and tidy impression for the royal visitors. He made his way to a magnificent triumphal arch that spanned the Kenilworth Road entrance to the town. Above the main arch on one side was a white banner which proclaimed "God Save the Queen" in gold letters, while on the other side of the structure a similar banner was emblazoned with "Hail Victoria". Over the side arches in scarlet letters on a gold background were the words "Loyalty" and "Welcome". The structure was crowned by The Royal Coat of Arms. By quarter past one in the afternoon, when the first sighting was made of the royal party approaching, the crowds had swelled in number and were in great voice. It was evident from the Queen's demeanour that she was well pleased by the arch creation that welcomed her into the town.

The royal couple and their entourage were escorted by the Stoneleigh troop of the Warwickshire Yeomanry riding their horses two abreast. The party was greeted by members of the Local Board of Health, each wearing a white rosette, who then joined the cavalcade at a sharp walking pace. The cortege made its way through the arch and passed the cheering orderly crowds lining the Kenilworth Road. Further on was a platform built by Mr William Ballard, a Leamington builder, which was decorated in the national colours and surmounted by seven flags, the centre one being the royal standard flanked by the union flags. The structure was inspected and passed by the town authorities to accommodate one and a half thousand people who paid 5 shillings for a front seat, three shillings for the middle compartment and two shillings for the upper section. On the opposite side of the road was similar structure that was erected by another local builder, Mr Thomas Mason, to accommodate one thousand spectators who also paid for the privilege of a seated vantage point. William decided to follow the sound of clattering hooves at close range in order to experience as much of the day as possible. His example was matched by a great number of spectators that formed an ever-increasing ribbon of people following the royal party.

Passing Beauchamp Square, the royal procession turned onto the Parade where another platform had been erected by Mr Ballard under the directions of the "Queen's Visit Committee" for two thousand three hundred schoolchildren of all denominations. As they passed Christ Church, the chapel that served as a focal point at the head of the main street, Lord Leigh directed the Queen's attention towards the children dressed in brown capes, bonnets and caps. The children were singing a well-rehearsed rendition of the national anthem at the top of their voices, but this attention from the monarch led them to lose their discipline and join in the enthusiastic cheering that surrounded them. By this point William found himself in the middle of a tightly packed throng of people with hardly any room to move his arms. It was at this point that he decided to check the time on his pocket watch and was hit by the realisation that his watch was gone. His heart sank as he was struck by the fear that it might be lost for ever. William, in an increasingly aggressive tone, started asking the people around him, "Have you seen any pickpockets?" All his enquiries met with a negative response and he felt a sickening feeling in the pit of his stomach. It was only the importance of the day's event that prevented his sorrow from drowning him in self-pity.

The town's elegant terraces along the Parade were all festooned with colourful bunting and flags, while cheering spectators occupied each and every window and balcony. As the Queen's carriage passed the highly decorated Regent Hotel, the platform erected by William between it and the Denby Villa Gardens came into view. The majority of the structure was taken by Mr Bishop who invited one hundred of the oldest and most deserving members of the town to appreciate the spectacle from this prime vantage point. Once the procession had passed, his guests were directed into the Regent Hotel ballroom where they partook of a substantial dinner. In the southern part of the town, a similar benevolent act was performed by Mr Wise who provided for one hundred and fifty members of the labouring class at Shrubland Hall, his family home.

William greeted his family with enthusiasm in the hope of disguising the disappointment of his loss. "Have you all enjoyed the day so far?" he enquired.

"Yes," was the chorus response. But Martha was not so easily convinced that all was well with William. It had been previously agreed that the family would return home at this point and William would return later to collect Martha to enjoy the evening activities in the town's gardens. Martha gave William a reassuring kiss on his cheek before making her way with the other members of the family back to their house.

William, now in sombre mood, continued to follow the flow of spectators down the Parade. The crowd was large but orderly as the royal cortege passed the Royal Pump Rooms. In order to gain a panoramic view of events, Mr Coxwell, a hot air balloonist who was stationed in the Jephson Gardens, launched his new balloon secured to earth by strong ropes. The balloon, which he had named "The Queen", became the centre of attention for the crowd until the arrival of the royal couple. This novel approach adopted by the balloonist soon drew the attention of Her Majesty and the Prince Consort who found his actions much to their amusement. After the procession had moved on, Mr Coxwell provided a vertical lift in the balloon basket for passengers who paid 5 shillings to experience the aerial view of the garden. William was quick to take advantage of this novel experience in the hope that it would distract him from the disappointment of the earlier event and lift his mood. "If you are enjoying this taste of flight," said Mr Coxwell in his best salesman's voice, "I will later be offering extended flight opportunities to a select few adventurers."

William found the aerial view provided by the balloon extremely stimulating and spoke with a degree of disappointment. "Much as was I tempted to accept your offer, sir, this evening I will be accompanied by my wife and I'm afraid she would not entertain the idea under any circumstances."

From the elevated balloon basket, William observed the royal procession continue its passage over the River Leam bridge, passing the parish church and entering the narrow width of Bath Street in the old town area. On reaching the High Street the royal carriage turned right under the railway bridges towards the former turnpike now called the Old Warwick Road. At this point the party was greeted by a choir formed by pupils from the surrounding settlements of Offchurch, Tachbrook, Whitnash and Ufton. When the party reached the precincts of the town the Stoneleigh troop was replaced by Captain Wise's troop of Yeomanry to form the escort to Warwick Castle. The royal "progress" became more speedy and the party moved rapidly towards their next engagement as guests of the Earl of Warwick.

Once the Queen's cavalcade had passed through the town, the occupants of Leamington entered a period of quiet contemplation. However, the local board had requested that the inhabitants observe the day as a holiday. All the pleasure gardens in the town, which in normal times were the preserve of the town's wealthier inhabitants, were opened free of charge for people to enjoy for the rest of the day, and musical entertainment was provided by various bands including the Grenadier Guards.

CHAPTER 12

A hot air balloon ride to Chesterton Windmill

William returned home to collect Martha for their first evening out alone together since the birth of their two month old daughter. William's mother had volunteered to stay with the children in order to allow the couple to enjoy the evening's activities. As they prepared to leave Martha turned to William and said, "Is there something worrying you, dear?"

"No, nothing that should concern you and spoil your day," replied William in a reassuring manner.

Martha paused for a moment before enquiring, "Do you have concerns about your pocket watch?"

William could not disguise a shocked expression. "What do you know about the stolen watch?"

"I am not aware of the watch being stolen," said Martha, "but I did wonder if you had mislaid it. I discovered it in baby Martha's cradle when we returned from watching the royal visit."

William could not hide his relief. "Oh, my goodness!" he exclaimed. "It must have slipped from my pocket when I leaned over her cradle." As the couple left the house in a happy mood and looking forward to an enjoyable evening together, William informed Martha about his unusual experience with the balloon pilot.

Mr Coxwell became a focal point in the Jephson Gardens at five o'clock when he prepared to leave for a balloon journey to wherever the wind took him. William and Martha joined the large crowd waiting to witness the

75

spectacular event. The "grand ascent" was to carry passengers who paid five guineas a head for the privilege. The first attempt to launch failed due to lack of lift and it was decided that Mr Coxwell should attempt the flight on his own, much to the obvious relief of his now very nervous would-be passengers. After eventually receiving its full complement of 30,000 cubic feet of gas from the Leamington gas works, the journey was able to commence and the balloon rose slowly drifting towards the spire of the nearby All Saints parish church. For a moment the watching crowd feared the worst as the balloon struck the spire. Martha clutched William's arm and let out a large gasp. But the ever resilient Mr Coxwell waved his cap to indicate that things were fine and he continued his flight.

The winds took his balloon away quickly in a south easterly direction flying over what appeared to be the completely deserted settlement of Whitnash and past the village of Harbury which was clearly visible in the distance. Although Mr Coxwell was thoroughly enjoying the panoramic view of the beautiful Warwickshire countryside, he realised that the limited amount of fuel available on board meant that he must look for a suitable landing site. In the distance, he spied for the first time the profile of the limestone constructed windmill at Chesterton standing on its elevated platform surrounded by open fields.

Mr Coxwell admired the distinctive design of the circular stone structure (that housed the millstones in a first-floor room) supported on six stone columns linked together by curved Roman-style archways. The appearance of the structure was enhanced by the use of stone string courses and stone window mullions. A lead dressed domed cap covered the building and this was surmounted by a decorative wind vane. The cap rested on a rotating winding gear which allowed the sails to be manoeuvred to take advantage of the prevailing wind direction.

An engineer friend had explained to Mr Coxwell how the round arch was an innovation introduced by Roman builders. The Romans realised that although stone has a strong compressive strength, its tensile strength is relatively poor. Using a flat arch formed by one piece of stone could only be used over a narrow opening or it was liable to bend and crack. Mr Coxwell knew that the curved arches of the mill would have been formed using a temporary timber centre to support the stones in place during construction. Once the keystone was inserted at the head of the arch, the intrinsic compressive strength of the stone allowed the individual pieces to form a strong self-supporting monolith structure to bridge the openings. The curved arch allowed the span of each opening between the columns to be increased to provide a greater unrestricted working area for the miller.

As the balloon approached, the miller's eldest son was lowering sacks of freshly ground flour down through a floor hatch on the rope pulley system to his brother who was receiving them at ground level. The younger brother was loading the flour sacks onto the bed of a waiting wagon ready for delivery to their customers. The horse-drawn wagon with wide rimmed wheels was the usual means of transport along the rough and rutted country tracks. During winter the surrounding country lanes often became extremely muddy and impassable by wheeled vehicles; at this time packhorses became the most suitable alternative for moving the heavy sacks. In order to keep the flour dry during rain or snow, the wagon was enclosed by a canvas sheet pulled taut to form a tent over a frame consisting of a series of bowed metal supports that were firmly secured to the wooden sideboards. After loading was complete, a hinged tailboard was lifted and locked closed to prevent the sacks from shaking off the wagon during transit. To complete the enclosure a pair of canvas curtains at the rear of the wagon, that were tied back during the loading process, were drawn closed.

The eldest boy was the first to notice the approaching balloon as he looked through the first-floor window. He dropped the open bag he was holding and was covered in a dust cloud of freshly milled flour while shouting in a high-pitched voice down to his brother, "Look what's flying towards us!" They immediately stopped their work and rushed to assist the balloonist who had started his descent and was producing a loud screeching sound as his basket started dragging along the ground. Eventually the ground resistance forced the skidding basket to keel over and come to a halt as the deflating balloon fell to the ground. The brothers held on to the basket while Mr Coxwell emerged relatively unscathed and thanked them profusely for their assistance.

"That journey was one of the most exhilarating of my ballooning career," declared Mr Coxwell whilst enthusiastically shaking the hand of each of the miller brothers. Long steel pins retrieved from the balloon's basket were driven into the ground and the balloon was secured for the night. "Now one more thing," inquired Mr Coxwell, "could I impose on you young gentlemen one more time by requesting the loan of a horse until I return with the means to collect my flying equipment tomorrow?"

The brothers nodded knowingly towards each other. "I'm sure we have a pony in our paddock which can be spared until tomorrow," replied the elder brother. "That's excellent," replied Mr Coxwell. "I will see you well rewarded for your invaluable assistance today."

When he eventually returned to Leamington later that evening there was still a large gathering of people, including William and Martha Gascoyne, waiting to hear about his adventure. Mr Coxwell, who loved entertaining an audience, introduced more than a little embellishment while recounting his journey in terms of a great drama. Emphasising the vulnerability of the adventure he exclaimed, "The course of my eventful mystery trip was determined by nature, and it was kindly terminated in a field close to the famous stone arched Chesterton windmill."

The end of Mr Coxwell's gripping story was greeted by loud applause and the listeners left in a good mood. The climax of the memorable day was a free fireworks display that lit the night sky over the Jephson Gardens which was packed to capacity. At the end of the evening's entertainment the cool Leamington air was filled with the smell of spent pyrotechnics as the crowd of people began to disperse. As William walked Martha home, he reflected on the day's events with a warm glow of satisfaction. "I believe our town has proved itself worthy of our royal visitors." With a degree of excitement in his voice he added, "How fortunate we would be if we could have a royal visit more often." Martha uttered a sound that conveyed her total approval of his sentiment.

CHAPTER 13

Opportunities for church building realised in Warwick

Architect James Murray suffered from poor health throughout his career and in 1860 it was decided by mutual agreement to dissolve the partnership of Murray and Pugin. Murray and his family relocated to Coventry where he established an independent architectural practice. William continued his association with both the former architectural partners to great effect. James Murray was very supportive of William as he initially undertook house building on a negotiated contract basis for wealthy clients, and then on a speculative basis as he developed a strand of his business as a property developer. Unfortunately the relationship with Murray was prematurely terminated when the architect contracted tuberculosis, the ubiquitous scourge of Victorian England, at the early age of thirty-two years, but by this stage William had gained valuable experience and had developed sufficient business acumen to sustain profitable residential developments.

William's business connection with Edward Pugin continued to serve him well. Edward's father, Augustus W. N. Pugin, had gained wide recognition for his design work for the Houses of Parliament in conjunction with Charles Barry. Augustus became a convert to the Church of Rome and had dedicated a significant percentage of his highly successful and nationally renowned architectural practice to ecclesiastic building for the Church in the Gothic Revival style. After his father's death in 1852

Edward took up his successful practice. The Pugin's involvement with the Roman Catholic Church was at a time when events changed the situation for British Catholics and their Church; in 1829 Parliament granted them full civil rights, including the right to serve in the legislature.

Events surrounding the Roman Catholic Church and the effects it had on a surge in church building was to the benefit of William. The Roman Catholic Church's building programme was stimulated in 1850 when a "papal bull" (a public decree) issued by Pope Pius IX reinstated the Catholic Church organisation in England, including parishes and dioceses. Much public concern was expressed at both national and local level concerning the papal bull. In conformity with the decree, Dr Ullathorne was enthroned in October of the same year as the new Catholic bishop of Birmingham, which was established as the diocese for the Catholic parishes in Warwickshire. Vocal criticism of these events came from a number of local Protestant clergy. Two meetings were held at the music hall in Leamington during November 1850 with the purpose of making representation to Queen Victoria about the perceived aggressive movement of the papacy. In Parliament, Lord John Russell in response to the strength of Protestant reaction in the country as a whole, introduced in February 1851, his Ecclesiastical Titles Bill in an effort to curb papal claims by legislation. The restructuring of the Catholic Church in England proceeded despite the resistance shown. In June 1873, *The Daily Telegraph* was able to report that the Catholic Church in England consisted of an archbishop and twelve bishops. In the thirteen Catholic dioceses there were 1,016 public churches and chapels and 1,621 clergy.

Whilst William took no interest in religious prejudice, he was prepared to make the most of the opportunities presented by the upsurge in building work associated with the Roman Catholic Church. William willingly undertook the building of a new Catholic Church of St. Mary Immaculate in West Street, Warwick, under the supervision of Edward Pugin. The foundation stone was laid by the Reverend Canon Jeffries of Leamington and the church was opened on Tuesday 12th June 1860. Pugin's design consisted of a nave, two aisles and a chancel. Local press described, "the style of the building was in decorative early English and it was built of Bath stone and red brick. The length from east to west was 86 feet and from aisle to aisle 45 feet. A bell turret crowned the roof near the west end and the whole height of the front was 78 feet". The success of a completed contract conducted between William and Pugin was to be repeated on a number of subsequent building projects.

In 1916, the attractive Warwick church built by Gascoyne was to witness the marriage of John Ronald Reuel Tolkien, the author who became famous for his fantasy novel *The Lord of the Rings*. Tolkien was born in South Africa in 1892 to English parents who had both died by 1904. Tolkien, a Catholic, was raised in an orphanage in Birmingham, during which time he fell in love with his future wife Edith Mary Bratt. Although the relationship was disapproved of by his guardian because Edith was a Protestant, this did not deter the young Tolkien. In 1911 he commenced studies at Essex College, Oxford, and during this time Edith moved to Warwick. Her house in Victoria Street became a place for many discrete meetings between the couple prior to their wedding.

CHAPTER 14

Creating training opportunities for apprentices

William was operating in a labour intensive industry and by 1861 he was employing seventy-two men. He claimed, "to be the only establishment in the town and the immediate neighbourhood where at all times experienced men in every branch of the building trade are constantly employed." At this time a typical builder only employed other trades as required during a project. By becoming the full-time employer of various tradesmen, William's business created the paradigm of a modern building company, a format adopted extensively by later building companies.

The skills William had learned during his apprenticeship made him supportive of training young people. His workforce included a number of indentured apprentices. William Richard Leach of Leamington Priors signed a typical indenture with the Gascoyne Building Company to be instructed in the art of carpentry and joinery over a period of three years. During his time he was to be paid 2⅛d. per hour in the first year, 2½d. per hour in the second year and 3d. per hour in the final year. In exchange, the apprentice agreed to serve his master faithfully and not to damage, waste, or unlawfully lend their goods. He further undertook not to commit fornication, contract matrimony, play at cards or dice table, to haunt taverns or playhouses, nor to absent himself from his master's service, day or night.

William's ability to offer opportunity to would-be apprentices was provided through the post he held as a churchwarden at Leamington parish church. When the church choir required new young members in February 1867, William and his fellow churchwarden Mr Walter Watson placed an advertisement in the local Leamington newspaper for a dozen respectable boys to be trained for choristers. In return for their musical services, the boys were to be offered a good practical education.

William was able to provide training for children of the poor by approaching local charities that were prepared to sponsor indentured apprentices. On 16th April 1868 he wrote to the trustees of the charity estate of Alderman Richard Lane, advising them that he was prepared to bind for five years a boy called Richard Aigne of Bridge Row, Emscote, in the Borough of Warwick. The indenture was signed between Richard, John his father, the trustees, and William, binding the apprentice to be taught the trade of a builder. The consideration paid by the trustees to William was £10 and the wage paid by William to Richard was agreed at 6 shillings per week in the first year, 7 shillings per week in the second year and increasing by 2 shillings per week in each of the following three years. Around this time a total of eleven boys were employed by William.

The apprentices were introduced slowly to their future trade. Initially their duties involved playing a supporting role to the time-served craftsmen. Fetching and carrying materials, together with sweeping up and keeping the working area neat and tidy formed a major part of the working day. William often reminded his apprentices that, "a good tradesman could be easily identified by the condition of his tools." An intrinsic part of the apprentice training was to learn how to use tools safely and keep them sharp. The services of a blacksmith could be relied on to provide good strong chisels, while "saw doctors" were skilled at sharpening and setting the teeth for the many types of saws used by the various building trades. The apprentice was required to ensure that no tools were lost and that they were kept well-oiled to prevent them rusting.

Whenever possible, William's apprentices were employed to save the company's costs by recycling materials, such as straightening bent nails so they could be reused. Salvaging building materials and reusing equipment was a practice often employed in the local construction industry. Many years before in 1850, when the Great Western Railway Company decided to erect a new station in the old town area, it acquired a site on the road to Warwick. The site contained a majestic terrace of high quality four-storey houses that had been built only a decade earlier. The existing properties called Eastnor Terrace were demolished and William attended the site on a number of occasions as the salvaged materials were sold for reuse. Much of the saved materials were acquired for a new housing development on a nearby site on the Tachbrook Road.

Although the apprentices in the Gascoyne company were not subject to any embarrassing initiation ceremony, they were often the butt of joke requests by older members of the workforce. New boys were often sent to collect a variety of "impossible" items:
"Collect a left-handed screwdriver for a left-handed person."
"Go to the store and get a pair of sky hooks for supporting the new shelving."
"Bring a glass hammer for work on a window."

"Go for a long wait for a sash window." Fellow members of the workforce often played along and it would take a while before the subject of the prank realised he had been fooled. Occasional amusing antics of this type helped to create a light-hearted atmosphere around the workplace. William's workforce was generally regarded as a happy and content group with a good degree of loyalty and commitment to their employer.

It was an established practice for apprentices to run errands for the tradesmen during a break time. One bold apprentice who had been the butt of a joke by an older member of the workforce decided to seek retribution. After biding his time the boy was eventually asked by his target to go to the local corner shop to buy his usual tobacco. The young lad returned to report, "There is none of your usual tobacco to be had."

The tradesman, keen to have a smoke of some type during his lunch break replied, "If none of it is available then anything would do." The mischievous boy soon returned again and handed the man a paper bag containing a pie. The bemused man inquired with slight of annoyance, "Why have you brought a pie?"

The boy responded in a slightly cheeky tone, "I was simply following the instruction you gave me, that if none of your usual tobacco was available then anything would do." The incident was the subject of much laughter in the workshop and the event was often recounted during conversations for the amusement of fellow workers.

CHAPTER 15

Incidents with young people

A handcart was often employed by William's tradesmen who needed to transport small quantities of materials or access ladders and other equipment from the workshop to the site where they were working. The task of pulling the cart invariably lay with the apprentices who were often required to make journeys over a number of miles along the shale roads. The white painted wooden cart consisted of a flatbed with side boards sign-written with the William Gascoyne company name. On each side the axle was supported on thirty-six inch diameter cartwheels with steel rims and wooden spokes. A wooden beam extended from the front and terminated with a handlebar which allowed the cart to be pulled along.

William's apprentices were sometimes required to work with the horses and wagons employed to transport the heavy loads of wrought stone and other weighty materials from the Gascoyne workshops to the company's building projects. To assist these animals in their tasks, collars were used to distribute the weight evenly around the horse's neck as it hauled the load. If space allowed, the horses were also used to distribute goods and equipment to where needed around the site. Although the horses were well cared for and their equipment was regularly checked and cleaned, incidents involving workhorses were not uncommon.

At about five o'clock in the evening on Tuesday 8th September 1863, a horse belonging to William's company became detached from the cart which it was drawing, when the bolt which coupled the shafts to the body of the vehicle had shaken out. The animal spooked and with the shafts still attached to it galloped furiously through several of the surrounding streets. It eventually rushed into the gas works in Priory Street where it had a narrow escape from falling into the bed of an old gasometer. The horse was eventually secured without causing or sustaining much injury and was returned to its owner.

An incident involving another of the Gascoyne workhorses occurred on the morning of Saturday 25th June 1864. Whilst hauling a heavy load of sand along the Mews Road at the back of Beauchamp Square, Leamington, the horse suddenly sank into the new sewer that had been recently constructed. During the preceding night some mischievous person had turned on the water supply that had been used by the builders during the construction work. The consequence was that the loose soil filled in over the sewer became saturated and turned into a form of quicksand. Attracted by the driver's cries for help, assistance was provided by Mr Owen of the Clarendon Livery Stables and several of his men. Although the horse was eventually extracted without sustaining serious injury, it was clear that in a very short time it would have been completely submerged, as the weight of the load prevented it attempting to free itself and was dragging it deeper into the mire. William was aware that his apprentices were clearly shocked by the incident and in order to console them he gathered them together. "Be assured that the care and kindness you have shown for the animals we employ does not go unnoticed and we will do all that is possible to ensure their wellbeing." William ensured that he personally thanked all those that had assisted the rescue and made it clear publicly, "That any person found causing such acts of vandalism would be dealt with severely."

There were occasions when a refractory apprentice rebelled against his master and broke the terms of his indenture. This often resulted in his arrest by the local constabulary and an appearance before the local courts. This was true for one of William's apprentices, Thomas Hawkes, who was charged with unlawfully absenting himself from the service of his master on 8th June 1863. The prisoner, an apprentice painter, pleaded guilty to the offence and was subject to sentence. At this point William addressed the court: "If the boy liked to go back to his work and make up the fortnight he had lost, I would be quite satisfied."

The defendant was grateful for the intervention. "I would be prepared to comply with this proposition."

William further stated, "I shall be quite satisfied if he will make up for the time he has lost and pay the expenses of these proceedings. Payments could be made by weekly instalments and he may work what overtime he likes in order to do so. He is a painter and he may soon do it." From the bench Mr J P Gubbins admonished the defendant who was discharged on William paying the court expenses of 19s. 6d. and Hawkes agreeing to repay the same to William by instalments of 2s. per week.

There were circumstances when William was not so sympathetic towards young people. In June 1866 Alfred Wooley, a ten year old boy, appeared before local magistrates charged with having stolen a brass tap, value 3s., from the Gascoyne Building Company. William was conscious of how pilfering could damage his business and was determined to deter further attempts. Despite being sympathetic to the child's poor circumstance, he was keen to publicise the consequences of such actions regardless of who the perpetrator may be. The defendant pleaded guilty in the hope of being granted leniency by the court. On the bench were Messrs Wheler and Gubbins who looked to make an example with the punishment they handed down. The boy was to be imprisoned for one day and to be privately whipped on his discharge.

CHAPTER 16

William becomes a public figure

William's quest to promote improvements and advances in the town's services and facilities for the wellbeing of its residents was a consistent theme. Late evenings were an opportunity for William and Martha to relax alone together while sitting in their comfortable armchairs of their first-floor drawing room. As he raked the fire ready to place more coal with tongs in the grate from the highly polished brass coal scuttle, William revealed, "I have decided that in order to pursue my objective to improve public health, I must achieve a greater public profile."

During the dozen years since the tragic loss of their son John, Martha was always fully supportive of William. She put down the pencil she had been using to draw a flower on her sketch pad and enquired, "What have you got in mind, dearest?"

William cleared his throat and continued. "It is my intention to stand for public office and pursue improvements through the Local Board of Health."

"I may be biased, but I cannot think of a more suitable candidate," was Martha's complimentary response, intended as a resounding endorsement of his proposal.

On 5th November 1861, William took a proactive step to have a personal influence in the administration and development of Leamington when he was elected to the Local Board of Health with the support of eight hundred and eighty-four voters. His experience in the construction industry was recognised by the board members and he was appointed to serve on the Highways, Waterworks and Improvements Committee. William regarded his service to the community extremely seriously and became a regularly elected member of the town's guardians. He was a very active member of the board, particularly in matters where he could apply to good effect his knowledge of building for the health and safety of Leamington residents. This included matters appertaining to a building's structural stability, its drainage and sanitary provision, together with controls over the use of combustible materials. He reminded his fellow members of the board, "that while enforcing that new houses should be duly inspected, they should not overlook grave matters affecting the security of life and property."

William was determined to establish himself as a fully integrated and active member of the Leamington community. Freemasonry membership seemed a very obvious way to William to expand his network of business associates and influence. In July 1862, the thirty-five year old William commenced the ritual ceremonies which culminated in him becoming a member of Guy's Lodge. The Lodge which held regular meetings in the Bath Hotel, Leamington, was composed of an assortment of local businessmen and traders who came together for their mutual advantage. William was a regular attender of meetings and kept himself informed of commercial activities taking place between Lodge members in the town. It was inherently recognised by the members of the Lodge that the fortunes of the town and their own were synonymous.

Members of the Lodge were happy to expand William's knowledge about Leamington's development as a spa town. Initial expansion was centred on the seven spa wells, found to the south side of the River Leam and proved to be financially rewarding for the property owners there. The desire by landowners to profit from development on the northern side of the river triggered a search for wells in that area. However, the substrata on the north side of the river only provided one suitable site for extracting spa water, on the land belonging to Mr Bertie Greatheed of Guys Cliff, Warwick. Erection of new pump rooms and baths on the site was successfully completed and opened in July 1814. The newly created facilities proved to be a commercial success up until the 1840s when the popularity of Leamington, along with other British spa towns, declined in the face of competition from the continent. The decline in demand for spa treatments resulted in the closure of the building with the intention of demolition and selling the site.

William believed the pump rooms with its assembly room was a desirable asset for the good image of the town. In an effort to preserve the property, William had attended a public meeting on 8th March 1861 at the Regent Hotel for the purpose of receiving a report of a committee appointed to form a company to be called "The Royal Leamington Spa Pump Room Association (Limited)". The company was established with a capital of £8,000 in 1,600 shares of £5 each, of which William bought ten shares. It was agreed by the directors to undertake a substantial refurbishment of the existing building and add a Turkish bath and swimming pool.

Despite the effort and investment, the relaunched pump rooms failed to become a profitable concern. At the annual general meeting of the company held at the Royal Pump Rooms on 9th September 1862, William's concern led him to hope that he and other members could render further support and enquired, "Would it be any advantage to the company for shareholders to give their sums subscribed as donations?"

He was advised by the chairman, "The company was able to issue more shares and that the suggested action was not required."

However, the positive view about the viability of the association proved to be misplaced and the response to William's proposal was reassessed. At a special meeting of the company on 20th October 1864, Mr Gascoyne was thanked for "the very liberal offer" he had made by presenting his shares to the company. In response William stated, "he intended to hand over the shares without publicity, for he went on the principle that he owed the town a great deal, and that if he could in any way or shape benefit the town it was his duty to do so." Mr Shepard on behalf of the association hoped, "that the good example of Mr Gascoyne would be followed by others." The pump rooms, however, did not achieve the commercial success anticipated by the association and by 1867 the property was sold to the Local Board of Health.

CHAPTER 17

Prestigious building contracts in Leamington Spa and Warwick

William's growing business success and confidence in the Leamington housing market encouraged him to approach the Willes family and buy numerous undeveloped building plots, fronting the streets laid out to Edward Willes' masterplan for the new town. In 1859 William had obtained approval from the Leamington Local Board of Health for the first of twelve expensive villa-type properties that he erected during the following decade along the fashionable Newbold Terrace. From this time advertisements offering Gascoyne houses for sale started to appear regularly in local Leamington newspapers. William's growing reputation and business acumen enabled him to quickly secure clients for the building plots and recoup his land cost, while simultaneously securing the building contract.

William's reputation for reliability and quality meant that his services were now in great demand and he was able to run various substantial contracts simultaneously. In August 1861 he had been instructed by a local architect, Mr Bouleous, to build an elegant mansion on the Campion Hills for Mr William Adams. The property called Newbold Beeches consisted of a suite of reception rooms, eighteen bedrooms, two bathrooms, together with a cottage and stabling. William's stonemason skills were employed to create the attractive ashlar stone facade which, from its elevated position, overlooked the extensive Newbold Comyn estate of the Willes family. The manner in which the contract was conducted, together with the quality of workmanship was of paramount importance to the client in order to obtain approval for the scheme from these influential neighbours.

William was able to demonstrate his skills again using ashlar stone when he undertook the building of a Leamington mansion on the prominent corner plot of Beauchamp Square. The site was situated at the top end of the Parade, the main road running north from the River Leam through the new town. The square had been laid out during the earlier building boom in the town in accordance with the town plan prepared for Edward Willes and was based on similar proportions to that of Grosvenor Square in London. On 16th June 1862, William submitted an application on behalf of Mr Robert Hobson for erection of a house known as Beauchamp Hall. The Hobson family took possession of the mansion in January 1864, and on the evening of Tuesday 19th a grand ball was given. The very beautiful and costly decorated rooms were illuminated with gas light fittings and wax candles. The select company of distinguished guests assembled in the spacious and elegant drawing room where two magnificent glass chandeliers were suspended from the ceiling. The guests were feasted from a table which was profusely loaded with the richest delicacies, the most prominent dish being a boar's head.

There was no barrier to the type of work that William undertook and his client base came from an increasing variety of sources. In September 1864, William commenced additions to the Assize Courts at Warwick, which involved the erection of a suite of three rooms at the rear of the existing building to provide accommodation for members of the bar, jurors and witnesses. A corridor 7 feet wide was provided from the back hall with which both courts connected to the barristers' room which measured 29 feet by 19 feet. Also connected to the corridor was the waiting room for jurors which measured 20 feet square, and the room for witnesses, which measured 20 feet by 20 feet. The contract was completed by February of the following year for the total cost of £800.

The most striking of the Newbold Terrace properties built by Gascoyne was a mansion designed by Edward Welby Pugin. On 20th March 1869 William completed the purchase of a prime plot on the corner of Newbold Terrace and Newbold Street from Emily Willes and sold it on again the same day to Major Thomas Molyneux-Seel. He further contracted with him to build on the plot a grand Gothic-style villa for the sum of £20,000. It was designed to be one of the most prestigious residences in the town overlooking the beautifully landscaped Jephson Gardens. On 22nd November 1872, *The Building News* journal published a detailed description of the completed property: "The staircase was 10 feet wide and constructed entirely of stone, with handsome marble columns supporting the roof. On the ground floor there was a drawing room 89 feet long by 18 feet, and a dining room 28 feet by 18 feet. The first floor included a chapel, a billiard room, thirteen principal bedrooms, three dressing rooms and a bathroom. The third floor contained seven sleeping apartments for servants". In deference to a Harrington ancestor of Molyneux-Seel, the name "Harrington House" was adopted for the villa in 1876. Sadly, in 1967, the majestic building was demolished to allow redevelopment of the site for the Royal Spa Centre.

CHAPTER 18

National and local labour disputes

William's humble beginnings and his background in the building trade made it easy for him to empathise with his employees and he was often understanding and sympathetic to their needs. In 1859, carpenters, masons and bricklayers went on strike in London in order to achieve the right of combination (The Combinations of Workmen Act 1825 prevented trade unions from collective bargaining for better employment conditions) and secure a nine-hour working day. This was followed by a lock-out of building operatives in London. Attempts were made to engender support for the dispute in other regions of the country. On 26th August 1859, Thomas Grant Facey and William Cremer, two delegates appointed by the London Conference of the United Building Trade Society, addressed around two hundred and fifty workers connected with the Leamington building trade in front of Milverton Chapel. They informed the meeting of the various causes of the strike in London and requested subscriptions towards the support of the strike. At the conclusion of the meeting a resolution was proposed by James Meredith, a local plasterer, that the operatives of Leamington that were attending this meeting pledge themselves to support the men of London in their contest with their employers. It became evident to William that local Leamington building trade operatives like those in the capital were prepared to combine to support applications for improved conditions of employment.

During the early part of 1861, a request to reduce the hours of labour by finishing work at five thirty instead of six o'clock in the evening without a reduction of wages was made by the building operatives in Leamington through a circular letter to the employers. On 2nd May a meeting was called by the master builders of the town at the Temperance Hall in Warwick Street at which it was unanimously decided to reject the request from the men. A subsequent meeting of the operatives was held in the same hall the following evening at which, in response to the employers' decision, it was decided to establish a representative committee of all building trades. This would have the power to act as a whole body, except in the extreme case of striking. The meeting approved a further proposal that the employers be approached again in the hope that they would reconsider their decision, with a warning that the operatives would use all moral means to obtain what they desired. The Gascoyne company was regarded as the dominant builder in the town and an extremely courteous letter was sent to William by the operatives' representative committee to request a meeting with the employers on the following Wednesday. William immediately issued a brief note to the other building employers informing them of the request. The employers' collective response to the invitation was to reject it on the grounds that they did not wish to acknowledge a combination of men.

The *Leamington Courier* newspaper contended that a subversive external influence was involved in directing the actions of the operatives and made reference to a letter from a Mr Potter of the Association for the Building Trades in London, which encouraged the immediate establishment of a branch for building workers in Leamington. The newspaper suggested that in pursuance

99

of this outcome, a copy of the London association's rules and cards were provided to the meeting. In an attempt to defuse the situation, William's response to this strong editorial criticism was to request that a letter of his be published in the next edition of the newspaper, where he explained fairly the positions of the two parties, which he said "was not irreconcilable." He suggested that "the operatives' objective was simply to put the men in the town on equal terms with the men in most towns of England." He further stated that "the proposition put forward by the operatives had been misnamed a strike and this had put their cause in an unfavourable light." William maintained that "the employers had little to fear from an association of the men, this was because the town depended chiefly on speculative ventures and this placed employers in a position of strength." He warned that "if for any reason the employers decided to withhold their entrepreneurial input for a period of time, it would compel two-thirds of the employed to break up their homes and seek employment in other towns." He suggested this view might prove to be prophetic in relation to future disputes.

The majority of the building employers failed to submit to the men's demands and the disunity amongst them resulted in each being left to settle with their employees as they thought would best fit their own circumstances. On Saturday 11th March 1861, William's foreman presented him with a petition signed by over ninety of his employees requesting alterations to their hours of employment. Their request was to commence work at six o'clock on Monday morning instead of seven, to finish work on Saturday at four o'clock instead of five and to finish at five thirty instead of six on the other five nights.

After spending a day considering the operatives' document, William responded with a pragmatic approach: "I will accede to the request in full, on condition that the operatives agree to follow my regulations for the Gascoyne building firm." He presented a document to his foreman for the men to consider. William's proposal was, "An hour would be stopped for any man arriving more than five minutes late for work without a reasonable excuse being given." A ban was imposed on drinking alcohol or smoking in any part of the workplace. Tradesmen were to work from seven in the morning until five thirty in the evening at all times when the work was inside, and the dinner break was to be half an hour. The reasonable and progressive nature of William's plan was accepted unanimously by his workforce without any wish to alter it.

CHAPTER 19

Associations with the church

The manner in which William performed his duties while building the Roman Catholic Church of Saint Mary Immaculate in Warwick was very much to the satisfaction of Canon Jefferies. The two men continued to work together in a fruitful symbiotic relationship on almost all the work of any significance which the Church undertook in Leamington Roman Catholic parish over the next two decades. On 3rd December 1861, William presented plans to the Leamington Local Board of Health for alterations to Saint Peter's Roman Catholic Chapel in George Street, Leamington. The application was met with a tardy response, and at a meeting of the board held two weeks later William used his position as a member of the board to criticise the delay in sanctioning the plan. "I maintain this is being done in contravention of the Act of Parliament and the by-laws of the board. I contend that if the board continues to do so, I will proceed with the work and take the responsibility upon myself. I am no Roman Catholic and my principal object in this case is an individual interest." His strong personal stand for the proposal at this time further strengthened his business relationship with the Catholic Church in Leamington.

On 15th April 1862, the Leamington Local Board of Health approved plans drawn up by Mr Henry Clutton of Burlington Street, London, and submitted by William for a new Catholic Church in Dormer Place. The foundation stone of the church of St. Peter Apostle was laid on 1st

May of the same year by Bishop Ullathorne. The building work was completed by William at a cost of £6,121 and opened on 18th August 1864. The exterior of the church was red brick, relieved by bands of Warwick stone with dressings of Bath stone.

A further Henry Clutton design for a house adjoining the new Leamington church was sanctioned by the board on 16th June 1863. The church, together with the presbytery, built for £1,637, provided William with further opportunity to work with an architect of some renown. Clutton had already achieved distinction as an architect, for in 1856, together with William Burges, he had won an international design competition for the Notre-Dame-de-la-Treille Cathedral in Lille, France. Although that project was not executed, (the contract was given to a French architect), Clutton's talent was given further recognition in 1867 when he was requested by Cardinal Manning, Archbishop of Westminster, to submit plans for the proposed London Roman Catholic Cathedral in Westminster.

Although undertaking a substantial amount of work for the Roman Catholic Church, William was a practising member of the Church of England and regularly attended Sunday service at the Leamington parish church of All Saints. He became a churchwarden in June 1865 at a critical time in the history of the parish church, which had undergone substantial rebuilding work. However, the unfinished state of the building was the subject of concern, particularly the weakness and instability of the roof, which had been examined by a number of architects and builders, including William. The concern proved justified during a church service on the evening of Sunday 4th February

103

1866, when a thunderstorm made the roof vibrate and almost created a panic amongst the worshippers.

The frightening incident demanded urgent action and on 9th February William, together with his fellow churchwarden, announced in a public notice that, "the parish church was to be closed on the following Sunday until further notice." The action was sanctioned by the Bishop of Worcester who advised that, "the Publications of Banns and Marriages will take place at the temporary iron church until the rebuilding of the south transept and the putting on of a permanent roof is complete." At a vestry meeting held on Thursday 5th April 1866, the chairman, Mr Stanley, proposed that Mr Gascoyne be re-appointed as parish churchwarden. He stated, "William is worthy of our confidence, as he has always performed a safe and independent role." The vestry members agreed as the material fabric of the church was now in such an unsatisfactory state that William's practical knowledge would be invaluable. The meeting unanimously approved that William be reappointed and he served as the vicar's representative during the course of the remedial work undertaken by Coventry builder, James Marriott, which was completed in November 1868.

During 1874, St. Paul's Church, Leamington, was built as a new Church of England parish church in close proximity to the Gascoynes' property in Willes Road. Although William was not involved in the construction of the building, nor a regular attender at the new church, he once again demonstrated his generosity by donating a beautiful baptismal font. It was skilfully produced in his stonemasons' workshop and consisted of a lead lined bowl carved from Bath stone supported on four marble columns resting on a stone base.

In addition to being a devoted Christian, William was very patriotic and liked to demonstrate the fact whenever possible. Each year he celebrated St. George's Day, which coincided with the birthday of William Shakespeare, Warwickshire's greatest son. On Thursday 23rd April 1874, William organised a trip to Stratford-upon-Avon with a party of Leamington ladies and gentlemen, totalling twenty-six in number. When the visitors arrived they found the town bedecked with bunting and flags in celebration. As part of the day's event, William had prearranged a group tour of Shakespeare's birthplace, the museum and the school Shakespeare had attended. The party then visited Holy Trinity Church where Shakespeare had been christened and in which he was later buried. William Gascoyne's ten year old daughter Juliet placed a floral cross on the grave in a simple and touching ceremony, witnessed by some of the members of the Corporation of Stratford. The group's return to Leamington was scheduled to arrive for a six o' clock dinner served at the Crown Hotel. Grace was said by William before the meal and the bill of fare was appropriately illustrated by quotations from Shakespeare.

CHAPTER 20

A caring employer learns about the Coventry ribbon industry

William had become the archetypal modern building contractor, moving away from the traditional practice of independent tradesmen being employed to complete buildings. Now his various trades were integrated into a single building company and William was directly employing well in excess of one hundred workers. William was regarded as the leading representative of the building employers in the town and was a prominent figure during trade negotiations with the building operatives. There was great respect for his considerable knowledge of building matters, his business acumen and his honest concern for the advancement of his hometown as a desirable place to dwell.

On Wednesday 23rd July 1862, a bricklayer called John Moore fell from one of William's new villas being constructed in Newbold Terrace, Leamington. Timber scaffolding poles and planks, secured with skilfully tied ropes, provided a working platform for the stonemasons and bricklayers building the superstructure. Moore was working at roof level at an elevation of nearly 20 feet and fell across the timbers of the first floor, which somewhat broke his fall, but did not prevent him being precipitated to the ground. He sustained serious internal injuries and was taken to the local Warneford Hospital which provided a medical service to the local community on a voluntary basis.

This unfortunate incident motivated William in 1863 to become involved in organising a sick fund society for his employees. The society was run by an elected Committee of Management, of which William was a founding member and held the post of treasurer. The early days of their efforts were almost disheartening as the entrance money was all expended in relief to three fellow workers who were sick. William gave a reassuring address to the society's committee meeting held in the company's stonemason workshop. "If the survival of the fund can only be achieved by a loan, then I believe it is my duty to provide it." The members were encouraged by William's confidence and his financial support. Funds improved as the year progressed and the society eventually ended the year in a sound financial position. In recognition of their good fortune, the committee very generously agreed that a donation of £5 from the fund be given for the relief of the distressed of Coventry who were suffering greatly from the depression in manufacturing at this time. To this amount William immediately added a personal donation of two guineas.

The City of Coventry had emerged as the dominant centre of ribbon manufacture in England and William became familiar with the history of the industry during his meetings with James Murray. James had chosen to establish his architectural practice in the city after his move from London. The two men had established a sound business relationship together with a good friendship. Business meetings between William and James were often followed by relaxed friendly discussions during which William expressed an interest in learning about Coventry's recent history.

Pleased to try and satisfy his friend's curiosity, James begun to recount his knowledge of the city's ribbon manufacturing. "Ribbon weaving in Coventry began in the late 1600s and by the early 1700s it had become the main industry. Approximately half the city's population was employed in the ribbon industry with much of the work being performed as a cottage industry. Production was carried out mainly by women outworkers using looms in their homes and being paid by piecework based on their output. The imposition of import restrictions on ribbon had provided protection for the industry and induced a degree of complacency which inhibited modernisation."

William interjected, "I believe artificial barriers can only inhibit progress in a competitive market."

James nodded agreement and continued. "This became evident when the development and introduction of engine looms transformed the production of ribbon and led increasingly to the employment of male workers, who usually worked in a room on the top floor of their house called a 'topshop'. Further changes for the workers occurred with the introduction of the Jacquard loom in purpose-built factory buildings. Using punched cards to produce patterns, these looms could manufacture as many as eight ribbons at a time. The production of ribbon on a more commercial basis required fewer workers and the number employed in the industry declined to about a quarter of the city's twenty thousand population. Being unhappy with the situation created by industrialisation led some workers to react by burning down the first steam powered looms at Josiah Beck's factory in the city."

William spoke in a dismissive manner, "These Luddite-type actions were always doomed to fail in the face of progress."

James's tone became even more serious. "However, worse was to come for the weavers in 1860 when the Cobden Treaty abolished customs duty on imports of French silks which made French ribbons cheaper than Coventry ribbons. As a result the city suffered a terrible decline in the demand for Coventry produced ribbon. Many firms in Coventry were bankrupted and thousands of weavers and their families were left in dire straits. Many desperate weavers sold their possessions including clothes, furniture and even their looms. Some decided they were left with no alternative but to leave the city and emigrate to America or Australia."

That slump in the city's fortunes continued for several years and led to much suffering in the city. The miserable circumstances of Coventry's inhabitants received wide coverage in both local and national newspapers and relief funds were set up to provide them with help. The appeal to give support for the less fortunate received sympathetic support from both William and his workforce.

CHAPTER 21

Civic pride

William became increasingly proud of his town of residence, and on 16th May 1863 he wrote a letter to the *Leamington Courier* in which it was his contention that the Leamington residents enjoyed, "a well-drained, well-lighted and well-regulated town, approaching as near perfection as time and circumstances could allow it." In order to make the amenities of the town more widely available for its community, on 16th June 1863 William proposed, "The Local Board of Health should apply to the Lord of the Manor, Lord Alyesford, for permission to allow the public to use boats on the lower part of the River Leam below the Victoria Bridge." He further stated that, "I hope to see the provision of a small crane to lift boats over the weir in order to enable them to travel downriver as far as Warwick Castle."

Although the chairman welcomed the idea, he advised William, "It would be better to get the memorial from the town for the proposal." William took up the challenge and at a meeting of the Local Board on 21st July 1863, he submitted a memorial signed by upwards of five hundred ratepayers of Leamington, requesting the Board of Health to take some steps to admit boating on the lower part of the River Leam.

William pursued his campaign as an advocate for the healthy pleasure of boating on the river, and on 2nd May 1864 he wrote to the Local Board requesting, "An order of the board be given to putting a landing place at Adelaide Bridge and that the board give notice to the ratepayers that they are at liberty to boat on the river from Adelaide Bridge to the railway arches." On 24th May 1864, the *Leamington Courier* reported that the blockade of this section of the river had been lifted a fortnight previously and that boats had been placed on the water. At a Board of Health meeting during the following month, William was pleased to confirm that he heard from the surveyor's report that, "A landing had been made near the Adelaide Bridge and he was pleased to say that a number of ratepayers had availed themselves of the pleasure of boating."

By 1865 William's increasing business interests together with his expanding family led him to extend his house to provide more bedrooms, together with a self-contained suite of offices for his business. The business accommodation provided a comfortable reception room incorporating an attractive cast iron fireplace where, on cold days, a roaring fire was laid to welcome clients as projects were discussed and contracts agreed. A room to the rear provided a drawing office for developing the architectural practice within the company. In addition, a coach house was built to provide stabling for a horse and carriage. Martha was able to spend much of her spare time in a large conservatory built for her at the side of the house where she was able to propagate plants for her private garden which stretched along the property front on Newbold Road. A neatly cut lawn edged with a profuse range of gaily coloured flowers provided the perfect setting for tea on warm summer Sunday afternoons.

The improving financial circumstances for the Gascoyne family meant that they were now able to employ domestic staff, the first being a sixteen year old live-in house servant, Elizabeth Parrott, who hailed from

Leamington. By the end of the decade the family enjoyed the live-in services of Sarah Allsop, a forty-six year old cook from the nearby village of Cubbington, and Sarah Ann Bates, a nineteen year old house maid from Coventry. Joseph Cook, a thirty-one year old groom from Heyford in Oxfordshire, was employed to care for the horse and carriage that William had acquired to transport him between the various building sites he was operating simultaneously in the locality. When not required for business use, the carriage together with the services of the groom was available for Martha and other members of the family.

As William walked around Leamington, he noticed how the early attempts at planning the development of the town provided the pattern for future expansion. In the first half of the nineteenth century many streets were laid out during the initial development of the new town to the north of the river. As a result of economic depression in house building, the intended rows of terraced buildings to line these new streets were often only partially completed, or in some cases not even commenced. When later development of these plots did eventually take place, the grand terraced schemes of the earlier architects and planners such as John Nash, Peter F Robinson and William Thomas, gave way to infilling with detached Victorian villas which had become the vogue.

William understood that the evidence of early town planning that produced the uniform road system of Leamington distinguished the town from earlier established settlements, such as the neighbouring county town of Warwick which had developed over a long period of time in a random layout determined by land ownership and geographical factors. The layout of the Leamington

112

streets was set out on a grid system, with streets running in a northerly direction from the River Leam, crossed at a ninety degree angle by roads running east to west. The traffic in the town was never so great as to cause congestion and hold ups at the intersections, which was so often the case on Manhattan Island in the large metropolis of New York where the word "gridlock" was coined. During Leamington's growth the original village area and to the south of the river was referred to as "old town" and the new fashionable development to the north became known as the "new town".

The roads of the town were constructed of a stone sub-base and surfaced with a layer of compacted shale. The sound of a horse and carriage trundling along the road was a regular event and not unpleasant during normal times. However, an illness within a household could result in the familiar sound causing annoyance and efforts were sometimes made to muffle the noise with straw spread over the road surface. Only the plots that had been built on had a paved footpath along their frontage between the property boundary and the road. This resulted in a number of gaps along the walkways which proved to be a major inconvenience for the ladies of the town in their long dresses. On the other hand this was good news for the local cabmen who were kept well employed conveying the ladies to their social appointments. Roger Sharkey from Roscommon in Ireland came to Leamington in 1866 and became the proprietor of a successful livery stables and carriage hire business in Cross Street Mews alongside the Gascoyne workshops. Sharkey lived with his family at 64 Clarendon Street where standing in the bay window at the front of the house provided him with a clear view down Cross Street to his stables. Roger Sharkey became a prominent member of the local Catholic community, joining the Leamington branch of St. Vincent de Paul, a voluntary Catholic organisation providing practical assistance to those in need. William's work for the Roman Catholic Church, together with being a near business neighbour, meant that he knew Roger well and they became good friends.

Many years later Roger Sharkey met an untimely death as a result of injuries sustained in a horrific pony and trap accident in Leamington's main street. He was returning with his daughter and her husband from a Sunday afternoon trip to the village of Hampton-on-the-Hill where they had admired the panoramic views over the town of Warwick and its surrounding countryside. As they travelled from Bath Street and up the Parade, the pony was spooked by passing traffic and bolted, taking a sharp swerve towards a set of spiked railings that surrounded a large elm tree close to the obelisk at the entrance to Regent Grove. Roger tried hard to control the pony but the front of the trap caught the railings and he was thrown onto the spikes. He was taken to Warneford Hospital in a semi-conscious state but died soon after from the head injuries he had sustained. By the time of his tragic death, Roger Sharkey's profitable business had made him a very wealthy man.

CHAPTER 22

Hidden dangers and an accident on winter ice

During the first Tuesday in February 1864, William was talking to his carpenter foreman in his workshop when he was approached by a young man with the alarming news that a group of boys, which included his son William junior, had been involved in a fatal accident. William was filled with foreboding as rumour had it that one of the victims was named William and the son of someone associated with the building industry. William had a flashback to the events surrounding his son John's tragic accident in King Street. He murmured under his breath, "Oh God, not again." There followed a period of great uncertainty with much personal distress for William, until eventually further news came that the two individuals who had suffered an untimely death were thirteen year old Charles Perkins, the son of Mr Edward Perkins, nursery gardener of Adelaide Road, together with thirteen year old William Phillips, the son of Charles Phillips, a plumber and glazier of Brook Street.

Shortly after three o'clock a group of boys had ventured into the corner of a field belonging to Mr Hodgkinson, a Leamington coal merchant, located just off the new road to Warwick between Milverton Railway Station and the Portobello Bridge over the River Avon. An extensive pond measuring some twenty yards square and up to 10 feet deep had been constructed here to form a watering place for cattle. By Tuesday morning the bitterly cold weather had coated the pond with an apparently thick and secure layer of ice. Word had quickly spread among the young people in the town that the pond was an excellent place to slide.

The boys were confident that the thickness of the ice was sufficient to bear their weight but were ignorant of the depth of the pond and the existence of a spring which caused an irregularity in the formation and thickness of the ice. Mr Joseph Percy, a local newspaper reporter, was walking home from Leamington to Warwick when he noticed the boys' activity on the ice and he advised them to be extremely careful. However, their exhilarating sport was irresistible and the warning was disregarded by the boys. They had been sliding for some considerable time when suddenly, to the boys' consternation, the ice began to creak and crack under the feet of William Phillips and he disappeared into the freezing cold water.

Initially the remaining boys froze in horror and disbelief until eventually some ran off to find assistance while others bravely remained behind to attempt immediate rescue. The courageous Charles Perkins while endeavouring to find his friend moved towards the hole in the cracked sheet of ice, which gave way beneath him and he too sank into the freezing water. Another of the boys took a belt from around his waist and bravely knelt down on the ice while throwing the strap towards Perkins who managed to seize it. But the boy, finding Perkins extremely heavy, did not have the strength to haul him out of the water and was himself dragged into the pond. He had no alternative but to relinquish his hold of the strap and managed to scramble to the bank and safety.

The cries from the boys who went for help brought assistance from a Milverton roadsweeper who courageously dashed into the water and frantically searched around for bodies that had now sunk below the surface. The brave would-be rescuer became so benumbed by the cold that he was forced to give up his search and leave the water so that he could proceed home with haste to revive in front of a fire. As he departed, assistance arrived in the form of railway porters with ropes from nearby Milverton Station.

As news of the incident spread more people arrived, including a man who brought a drag hook from the nearby Portobello Tavern located on the bank of the River Avon at Emscote. The grab was not able to cut through the ice, but the use of a plank lifted with ropes and dropped heavily upon the surface of the pond, speedily broke up the ice. The drag was then used again and this time it brought the body of Phillips to the surface, and soon after the body of Perkins was recovered.

A passing horse-drawn vehicle was procured and in it the bodies of the two boys were conveyed to the Royal Pump Rooms at Leamington. The brother of Perkins, who had arrived before the boys were recovered, together with another man, tried in vain to revive the two cold motionless bodies. On arrival at the pump rooms medical attention was given by local surgeons Ralph A Busby and Charles W Marriott, who required the bodies be massaged while immersed in warm baths. This was done until it was evident that the practice was to no avail and that it was hopeless to persist. It was agreed that the boys were pronounced dead.

The coroner's inquest for the two boys was held in the pump rooms the following day where William Gascoyne junior was sworn in as a witness to the events. The coroner reported it was clear that there had been no foul play involved in the event and the jury recorded a verdict of "accidentally drowned". The incident brought back sad memories for William of events surrounding the death of his son John and he felt a degree of guilt about being relieved that this time it was somebody else's son and not his. Even so he empathised with the bereaved families and offered them his genuine heartfelt condolences.

CHAPTER 23

Improving public health with new sewage systems

During December 1861, the Queen's husband Prince Albert was suffering symptoms of fever and for some days the complaint was not thought to be serious. As the illness persisted the doctors in attendance began to feel anxious and it became evident that the prince would be confined for some time to the Palace. It was decided that no statement would be issued that would alarm the Queen or the public. By Wednesday 11th December, the fever had much weakened the patient and a bulletin was issued suggesting that the prince was suffering from a severe case of gastric fever but was expected to recover in due course. The prince, who had recently lost his relative the King of Portugal to a similar condition, may not have seemed so convinced. During Thursday the patient seemed stable and on Friday morning the Queen went for a drive in her carriage. On her return she was informed that the prince's condition had worsened and a bulletin was issued that he was now in great danger. In Leamington news of the prince in imminent danger was received by telegram on Saturday. On the morning of Sunday 15th December 1861, the sad news was received in the town that the Prince Consort had died of typhoid fever.

The shocking news created a wave of sadness throughout the population. Various places across the nation proposed the creation of a memorial in honour of the prince. Early in 1862 William published a letter in the *Leamington Courier* proposing that Leamington should erect a lasting memorial. He stated that, "in London the sum of £18,000 had been subscribed for this purpose and places such as Birmingham, Manchester, York, Chesterfield and Malvern were actively engaged in making arrangements to this end". William addressed the Local Board of Health and urged them, "A fund should be set up where all in the town could make a donation, large or small, with the intention of erecting a suitable memorial." He continued with an even greater tone of enthusiasm as he pointed out, "It has occurred to me that as directors of the Royal Pump Rooms have started renovation to the long neglected institution, I suggest that a suitable monument could form a focal point in the centre of the new building or in its grounds." In order to emphasise his good intention William announced, "I pledge the sum of £5 to the appeal if a fund is established."

Mr John Bowen, the Chairman of the Local Board, immediately volunteered his support. "I would be happy to receive funds and co-operate with any committee that was formed for the purpose."

In early July Mr Bowen reported to the meeting of the Local Board of Health, "There has been little response to the proposed project, and as a result I have let the matter drop."

William could not disguise his feelings in his voice. "I find it difficult to express my disappointment at the attitude of the townspeople towards the respected prince who has so recently visited Leamington." There was now a hint of anger as he spoke. "I feel that towns comparable with Leamington have taken a positive approach commemorating the tragic event, and I note a report in the press that at nearby Banbury a painted window has been erected as a memorial." With a degree of desperation he stated, "My five pounds is still ready and it is my contention to do all in my power to gain more subscriptions."

His words were received with enthusiasm by fellow board members and the chairman said, "I will call a town meeting during the coming week." It was promulgated that a meeting be held on Thursday 17th July 1862 at the town hall in High Street, where Leamington would consider the erection of some form of memorial.

Much to William's dismay he was required to attend an important site meeting for a potential building project in London and was unable to be present at the Leamington meeting. He prepared a letter of apology for his absence to be read at the meeting which confirmed his continued commitment to the project. In his absence the meeting went ahead and despite having been given widespread publicity, it attracted only a small number of Leamington inhabitants. Mr Bowen opened discussions at 11pm and asked, "Should we proceed with the business of the meeting due to the lukewarm response it has received?" It was generally agreed that there was little point in continuing without some sympathy from the public and Mr Bowen said, "I will take the chair for the purpose of dissolving the meeting." On receiving the result of the meeting, William reluctantly accepted that despite his efforts no lasting memorial for Prince Albert would be created in the town.

The death of the Prince Consort from typhoid, together with the circumstances surrounding the death of his son John, were both, William decided, associated with inadequate methods of dealing with the disposal of sewage. This provided motivation for William to promote and participate in the provision of adequate sewage

121

disposal schemes, both as a builder and a public representative in local government. In May 1863 he made a personal defence through the local press of steps that had been taken by the Local Board to improve the condition of the River Leam and of provisions made for the treatment of sewage, which had been the subject of criticism in the *Leamington Courier* on 9th May 1863. William propounded the advantages of the existing drainage system adopted by the town which he stated was, "Not a mere speculative scheme of one or two individuals, but had in all respects been carefully studied by scientific men and assisted with all the recent appliances of sanitary reform." Concern for the wellbeing of the inhabitants of Leamington and the diligent application of his duties ensured William's re-election to the Local Board of Health in 1864.

In March 1866, when further concern was being expressed about pollution of the River Leam by sewage, William was a member of the deputation sent to Surrey by the Leamington Local Board to report on the system which had been adopted by Croydon Local Board of Health of applying sewage to the land. Although the committee reported that the method used did provide a crop yield benefit to the irrigation farmers who received the sewage on their land with no unreasonable nuisance to the persons living in the neighbourhood, the majority view was that it was unable to give an immediate recommendation to adopt the Croydon practice. It was William, as the chairman of the Local Board of Health, who was largely instrumental in arranging for disposal of the town sewage in a like manner, when legal action was instigated in 1867 against the Leamington Board of Health by an injunction in the Court of Chancery for polluting the River Leam. An agreement was made with the Earl of

Warwick to receive the sewage of the district for a term of thirty years on condition that the Local Board delivered the sewage upon his land. William was subsequently responsible for laying the pipes conveying the sewage to Lord Warwick's farm and the irrigation works on the earl's land.

On the night of Friday 27th September 1867, a complimentary dinner was given for William at the Crown Hotel in recognition of his valuable services during his year as chairman of the Local Board of Health. Mr J Hadden acted as master of ceremony and about sixty persons were present, including some of the principal tradesmen of the town. William's health was proposed with great praise by the chairman, who stressed how, "William was always anxious for the welfare of the town and took great interest and devoted a lot of his time in forwarding the same." William acknowledged the compliment in appropriate terms, and after a number of further toasts were given the proceedings continued until a late hour.

William continued to pursue his mission promoting good sanitary conditions. By the mid-nineteenth century baths and water closets were becoming more commonplace in the nation's better quality houses. The wide range of sanitary products available was brought to the attention of the inhabitants of Leamington in October 1877 when an "Exhibition of Apparatus, Appliances and Articles of Domestic Use and Economy" was held at the Drill Hall, Adelaide Road, which was timed to coincide with the Sanitary Congress also taking place in the town. William commended the exhibition to his fellow builders. "It is the duty of all those involved in the maintenance and improvement of our environment to take an interest in novel products and inventions when they are introduced." Exhibitors included Messrs Leoni's gas cooking and hot water producing ranges, and Messrs Alcock's overflow flush pans. Among the novelties on display was the first crematorium ever shown in England, which was demonstrated by cremating dead rabbits.

William's work in the town, aimed at promoting advances in the field of public health, could not fail to impress General Ulysses Simpson Grant, the ex-President of the United States of America, when he visited Leamington in October 1877 as part of his highly successful tour of Europe. Grant had been the leader of the successful Union Army during the latter part of the American Civil War, and his high profile at the end of the War in 1865 led to an offer from the Republican Party to stand as their candidate in the 1869 presidential election. He was successfully elected as the eighteenth President of the United States and served two terms in that office during which time the fifteenth amendment of the American constitution giving black men the right to vote was ratified. Grant's travels eventually became a world tour and it was approximately two and a half years before he returned to the United States where he completed his autobiography before his death from throat cancer in 1885. William took great pride knowing that prominent figures like Grant were able to extend knowledge of Royal Leamington Spa beyond the shores of England.

CHAPTER 24

Labour relations and William's influence at the Leamington Board of Health

By the summer of 1864, disputes between building operatives and their employers were less local and occurred on a more regional basis. *The Builder*, a national publication for the building industry, on 2nd June reported that the Secretary of the Master Builders' Association of Birmingham had sent a letter to most building firms in the Midlands asking them to co-operate in forming a general association to take a united action to counteract the combined power of the operatives. This was a suggestion which William Gascoyne along with two other Leamington builders responded to positively. Fifteen districts were represented at a subsequent meeting of the "Midlands Counties Builders", when they adopted a resolution which required that every member should on or after 1st January 1865, when paying off any operative, issue him with a signed "discharge note". It was the duty of each member of the association to refuse employment of any operative, having previously worked for a member of the association, who could not produce a discharge note. A notice to this effect, dated 1st December 1864, was posted in the various workshops of the employers.

The action was widely condemned by the operatives at meetings held in Coventry, Nottingham, Leicester and Birmingham. Concerns expressed about the widespread opposition and pressure from the operatives resulted in a further meeting of the Master Builders of the Midland

Counties on 20th January 1865. A resolution was passed withdrawing the notice they had given regarding the discharge note, and through their association, to meet with the men to settle labour questions by the adoption of trade rules, and when differences remained to adopt a system of arbitration.

The proposal that the builders and their operatives should settle disputes through arbitration received active support from William. During the dispute over the discharge note, a deputation of four men representing all the building trades in the Leamington area had discussions with him and proposed the idea of establishing a Court of Arbitration for all trade matters. William undertook to distribute a circular to all the builders in and around Leamington urging them to take part in the establishment of a Court of Arbitration. He was profoundly disappointed that his invitation received only five responses and each of these made excuses for not participating. Despite the negative attitude of his follow employers, William continued to believe that industrial relations would be best served through consensus.

Although there was a lack of enthusiasm shown in Leamington, a Court of Arbitration was successfully established in some other West Midland towns, including Worcester and Wolverhampton. The benefits they produced led Leamington's trade unions, with William's endorsement, to promote the idea of a court in Leamington once again in late 1868. It was proposed that the court should consist of a board of annually elected representatives comprising six employers and six operatives, and its object would be to arbitrate on matters of wages, working rules or any other matters referred to it in order to prevent or settle any disputes. Each member would have one vote only and all running costs would be shared equally between the two groups represented. Once again the idea of creating a local Court of Arbitration failed to gain the support of the building employers and William's good intention of providing an amicable resolution of future trade disputes within Leamington's building industry were quashed.

During 1867 William's increasing business commitments together with his greater involvement promoting better labour relations within the building industry persuaded him not to stand for re-election to the Local Board of Health. It was agreed unanimously by the remaining members that the loss of William's influential leadership qualities would be to the detriment of the Local Board of Health during future meetings. The concern expressed proved to be well-founded when his influential controlling presence and diplomatic skills were sadly missed. During the monthly meeting of the board during September 1868, there occurred a disturbance which resulted in one member being summoned for assault in the local magistrates' court.

Before the magistrates was income tax collector Mr George Wamsley, who was unhappy about being required to stand down as a board member following recent elections. At a point in the Board of Health meeting when the retiring chairman, Mr Stanley, attempted to transfer the chair to the incoming chairman Mr Jones, there was continual disruption through verbal outbursts by Mr Wamsley as he protested about the way he had been treated. Even though he was advised by the chairman and supported unanimously by other Board of Health members that it was not the correct time to deal with his grievance, Mr Wamsley continued his harangue and seizing his hat, a felt deerstalker, threw it violently at Mr Thomas Muddeman, a prominent local coal merchant striking him in the face.

The action took everyone by surprise and several members suggested that Mr Wamsley ought to be taken into custody. After the chairman returned some calm to the meeting he advised Mr Wamsley that he should offer an apology before leaving. He offered an apology to both the board and Mr Muddeman, but the latter refused to accept stating that in addition to the assault he had been called, "a humbug and a two and a half penny bill discounter," when all he had said was, "Don't go on in such a blackguardly manner."

Mr Muddeman maintained that whdinile an apology was due to the board and may be accepted by them, as far as he was concerned he would take his own course. This was to result in Mr Wamsley's appearance at the magisterial proceedings the following day, during which the event was described as "an uproarious scene which would disgrace an Irish alehouse". Mr E Wheler, Chairman Magistrate, said the bench regretted that circumstances had led to such a case and at the same time they felt that some of the proceedings of the board had not been creditable to that body. The defendant pleaded guilty and was fined £2 plus costs of £1 8s 6d. It was the general consensus that if William Gascoyne, a fellow Freemason with Thomas Muddeman at Guy's Lodge, had remained a member of the Board of Health, the respect he commanded would have allowed him to arbitrate between the parties and defuse the situation.

CHAPTER 25

A regional market develops in Beckenham

After moving to live in Leamington, William continued to maintain contact with a number of friends and business contacts that he had established during his time in London. William visited the city often and was familiar with the problems of the capital's rapidly increasing population created by a booming economy. The growth in manufacturing had transformed Britain into the largest trading power in the world and London had become the most populated city in the world, placing great pressure on the city's environment and public health. Overcrowding and poor sanitation became a major problem when there was reluctance to spend money on public works. The River Thames in Central London was highly contaminated by the discharge of human sewage and industrial waste to such an extent that during the hot weather of July and August in 1858 it became known as "The Great Stink". William was pleased to learn that the situation was being addressed by a major sewer system designed by the civil engineer Joseph Bazalgette. Deaths from cholera outbreaks and other diseases were common and many residents who were able to do so migrated to more desirable healthier residential locations.

In addition to satisfaction that public health issues affecting the city were being addressed, William's entrepreneurial persuasion was excited by the commercial opportunities being presented in the developing residential areas emerging around the perimeter of London. It was during a social gathering with two former work colleagues, Robert Wilson and Frederick Collins, that William first became aware of a family who were intent on profiting from their land holdings in a Kent village not too distant from the city. The two friends lived in the County of Kent and William was eager to know more information about this village and the circumstances of the property owner.

William asked his friends, "What can you tell me about the background of the land in the village and its ownership?"

Robert took the lead in providing details. "Profit from land, particularly for the Cator estate, was a driving force for the residential development in the village called Beckenham. The Cator family fortunes had been established during the eighteenth century by John Cator, originally from Herefordshire, who had in 1748 established the business of John Cator and Sons, timber merchants in Southwark, London. The success of the business allowed his eldest son, John, to purchase the Lordship of the Manor of Beckenham in 1773. The further purchase of a cluster of farms in the area established a sizable estate and a fitting mansion was built called Beckenham Place."

Frederick, keen to contribute, took up the story. "When John Cator junior died he left no surviving children and the estate passed to his nephew John Barwell Cator, who in 1813 purchased Woodbastwick Hall, Norfolk, in order to pursue his sporting interests."

"Yes, that's right," Robert interjected, "and within a few years he had amassed enormous gambling debts."

Frederick, a little annoyed that his account had been interrupted, continued. "Although the Cator family were the principal landowners in the Beckenham area, the family spent the majority of their time at the family home at Woodbastwick Hall. Beckenham Place was let to tenants and in order to raise funds John Barwell Cator obtained parliamentary approval in 1825 to develop his estate for housing. This allowed him to obtain substantial sums of money to satisfy his creditors through mortgages on the land without development commencing."

Robert interrupted once more and took up the story again. "The financial affairs of the Cator family were eventually rescued when John Barwell Cator's brother, Peter, persuaded him to transfer control of the Cator Beckenham estate to Peter's eldest son Albemarle. Peter lived on the estate and acted as agent for its affairs. In 1854 he arranged for land to be sold at a beneficial rate to provide a railway connection to the parish, which created a very profitable market of building plots for high quality housing."

William became increasingly interested in the information and enquired, "So is there now a frequent and reliable railway service between Beckenham and the capital?"

"Yes, there is the Mid Kent line," replied Robert.

Fredrick, who had taken up residence in Bromley, not very far from Beckenham, was eager to share his detailed knowledge of the village. "Road layouts for development are set out on the Cator estate, including Copers Cope Road to the north of Beckenham Station following the line of the Mid Kent railway. The roads are unmade and it is the responsibility of the plot owners to pay a share of the cost for maintaining the road and footpath to the road in front of their land." In a voice that contained a suggestion of warning, Frederick continued. "Leasehold building plots are sold with conditions attached which dictate the target market for the occupants. A typical conveyance excludes the use of the land or buildings from being used for the purpose of the business or occupation of a schoolmaster, schoolmistress, boarding housekeeper, auctioneer, estate agent, or any trade business or manufacture of any kind."

It was becoming evident to his two friends that William was tempted with the idea of risking a speculative building venture when he asked, "Do you have more details about the building plots on offer in the village?"

"Yes indeed," said Frederick, pleased at his friend's continued interest. "Initially plots of half an acre were laid out for substantial villa-type properties, but later plots of a smaller area were also available in line with changing demand."

Robert returned to the conversation almost with the air of a salesman. "The provision of housing for the upper classes, together with a good train service to the City has inevitably marked out Beckenham as a prime location for commuters." William thanked his friends for their valuable information and thought to himself that this would be a business opportunity not to be missed.

CHAPTER 26

The family business branches out

The decade up to 1870 had witnessed strong demand for property in Leamington and the housing stock in the town increased by twenty-seven per cent. Although the housing stock growth rate reduced to seventeen per cent during the following ten years, the population growth was even less at ten per cent, producing an oversupply of property that resulted in a slump in the local market. Despite these local trends, William realised that an expanding national market for houses, combined with the improving means of transport and communication, provided opportunities further afield for profitable speculative residential development.

The slowdown in Leamington's population growth at this time coincided with a booming population increase in the Beckenham area of Kent which had risen by over fifty per cent during the same period. There were fast improving railway links developing within the area, and the population increase was substantially due to the ease with which people could commute into London from Beckenham. William was quick to recognise that there was a strong similarity with Leamington in the way in which Beckenham was growing rapidly during the nineteenth century from a small village into a substantial town.

It had always been his intention that his sons would play a leading role in the family business. His eldest son,

James, was now eighteen years old and William believed that the skills he had already developed were sufficient for some of the company's responsibilities to be delegated to him. William junior was sixteen years old and was also becoming increasingly active in the company. In addition to increasing his knowledge about building techniques, he was showing promising design and draughtsmanship ability.

William decided to call a formal business meeting with his two eldest sons in his office to discuss plans for the future of the company. Sitting in a formal manner around a table in the company office, William addressed his sons in a serious voice. "I have spent some time researching new markets for expanding our building activities. In order to achieve this, it is essential that you both take more responsibility. My contacts in London have been advising me of the opportunities for builders and developers around the perimeter of the capital, created by fast and frequent train services. We have already proven that we can successfully complete profitable individual contracts in London and other remote locations. It is my intention to use our experience and expertise to create a permanent division of our business located to the south east of London where I have been introduced to a landowner who wishes to profit from property development of his estate."

"How do we fit into this plan?" James enquired.

William expanded on his ambitious plan. "James, I know that you are thinking of settling down and I believe you are at a point where you could successfully run a branch of the company's business. It occurred to me that you could take the opportunity to combine adopting a senior role in the business while establishing a family home in a pleasant residential location."

"That certainly presents a desirable proposition," James responded. "But how will this affect William junior?"

William turned to his younger son. "William junior is proving to be a useful member of the team and I hope that he will be able to help consolidate the already well-established Midland based activities of the business." After further detailed explanation and discussion, the proposed expansion scheme met with everyone's satisfaction and William agreed to formalise their involvement in the business by forming a trading partnership with these two sons.

In 1867 the Gascoyne company took the bold decision to become a multi-centre enterprise when it established a branch of the company in Beckenham, Kent. As agreed, the management of the business in Beckenham was devolved to William's oldest surviving son, James, who moved down to Kent and lived in a hotel on the South End Road while overseeing the initial construction activities of the company in the town. The intention was that James would move to the area and become a permanent resident once the company had become more established.

The Gascoynes' first building plots in Beckenham were acquired as leasehold from the Cator estate in Copers Cope Road in 1867. The initial Gascoyne development in Beckenham's new town was marred by a tragic event on Tuesday 13th August 1867. George Barnside, a fifteen year old boy employed by the company, fell from the scaffold of one of the new houses being built. The fall resulted in a horrific injury to the lad, whose thigh was broken in two places. He was immediately taken to hospital on a police stretcher. Unfortunately, after examination at the surgeon house, it was decided that amputation was the only course of action. It was one more case to add to the poor health and safety record of the building industry. Alongside the mining and the fishing industries, building proved to be a highly dangerous working environment.

Despite this unfortunate incident, James managed the company's affairs well in Beckenham and the Gascoynes purchased further building plots on a similar basis from the Cator estate in Albemarle Road. The company built villa properties very similar in style to those that had proved desirable and financially rewarding in Leamington. This tried and tested business model again proved to be successful and the company started to see good financial returns. Now William's business advertisements for the company in local directories proudly announced that Gascoyne houses were available in Leamington Spa, Warwickshire and Beckenham, Kent. The Gascoyne company built a series of shops close to the bridge by the railway station to serve the needs of the rapidly expanding Beckenham community. William told Martha, "Our plans for our family and business are nearing fruition and we can feel a sense of pride in our achievements."

CHAPTER 27

Labour demands and court disputes

William's relationship and understanding of his workforce made him aware of the gathering discontent existing within the construction industry and the radical attitudes developing from this. During February 1869, the Leamington Lodge of the Operative Bricklayers' society requested sanction from their trade union to turn out on strike, should it be required, for 6d per day more wages in order to bring their wages in line with the men of the surrounding district. The return votes from a union ballot showed those in favour of the proposition were seven hundred and fifty-three, with seventy-two against. It was resolved by the union's executive council that the Lodge apply to the building employers for the parity in pay.

William's men were engaged on building the new Leamington Central Post Office in Priory Terrace. The building was being constructed on land purchased by the government from the vicar of All Saints parish church, the Rev John Craig. The design of the stone-faced building was produced by Mr Williams, architect to the Board of Works. It was a project suited to William's stonemason skills and his successful contract figure for the building work, excluding the interior fittings, was £2,300. It was William's intention to resolve the industrial dispute as quickly as possible in order to complete this prestigious government contract.

A communication from the operatives was sent to the Leamington building employers demanding that an additional 6d. per day to provide a new rate of 5 shillings per day, should be paid to all bricklayers, with a request for a reply confirming their compliance by Friday 4th June 1869. A special meeting of the men was held at the Temperance Hall on the Friday evening in order to study the response and decide upon further action. The meeting was informed that the only response received was from William Gascoyne and he had done so in a positive manner. It was resolved that each man on receiving his wages on the following day should ask his employer if he is prepared to grant the rise and, if not, to strike on Monday morning. On Saturday 5th June it was reported that eight other Leamington builders had joined with William to agree to the wage increase. William completed the Post Office contract successfully and the telegraph clerks took possession of the building on 29th January 1870. The prestigious new Leamington Central Post Office building opened to the public on 19th March of the same year.

The success of the working rules introduced by the Gascoyne company convinced William that this method of cooperation between employers and employees was the way to smooth future relations within the construction industry. It was a philosophy he propounded to others wherever possible. In June 1870, William Gascoyne and five other Leamington building masters signed an agreement with seven representatives of the employees, which formed the "Working Rules for the Regulation of Master Builders and Bricklayers of Leamington". These stated that the working week was to be a total of fifty-six and a half hours in the summer period, reduced to fifty and a half hours during the six weeks before and after

Christmas. The average workman was to be paid 6³/₈d. per hour, and overtime was to be paid at 8d. per hour. Suitable storage sheds and a mess room for the men to eat their food were to be provided in builders' yards and on building sites. For jobs more than ten miles from Leamington, provision was to be made for the men to return home once a week, and on country jobs lodgings were to be paid for by the employer.

It was further agreed that payment of wages would commence at one o'clock and a minimum of two hours' notice, or payment in lieu, was to be given by either the employer or the employee. A maximum age of seventeen was placed on first-time entrants to be apprenticed to the trade and no master was to take more than one apprentice in two years. These rules were to remain unaltered for a period of three years. At this time some trade associations were also proactive in providing welfare for their members. A system of ticketing was operated by a number of hospitals for controlled inpatient admission. "Subscribers" paid an annual fee in exchange for the right to recommend patients to the hospital whom they provided with a ticket. Indicative of this trend towards providing welfare was the action of the Friendly Society of Operative Masons, who in 1870 were subscribers to Leamington's Warneford Hospital in return for recommendation tickets for the use of its members.

William knew that the building employees were not unique in their aspirations, and he was alert to the fact that at this time Labour movements were being established in other industries. Locally, an agricultural workers union was established, largely due to the leadership of Joseph Arch from the village of Barford, about six miles from Leamington. Arch had only three years at school before starting work at nine years old. He developed an all-round agricultural ability and became a skilful hedge layer. The Arch family had lived in Barford for three generations and owned their cottage in Church Street. This secure domestic base enabled Joseph to journey considerable distances to find work. During his travels he became familiar with the poor living conditions suffered by agricultural workers. He married in 1847 and settled in Barford where he had seven children while becoming a Primitive Methodist preacher. It was here that he was approached by fellow agricultural workers appealing to him for support in their cause for better conditions.

William was aware of Joseph Arch's emerging influential prominence and followed his movements with growing interest. On 7th February 1872, Arch addressed around two thousand farm workers at a meeting held in front of the Stag's Head public house in Wellesbourne, a village approximately four miles from his home. This was followed by a gathering of agricultural workers from South Warwickshire in Leamington on 29th March 1872, to form the Warwickshire Agricultural Labourers Union. The National Agricultural Labourers Union was established exactly two months later with forty-six year old Joseph Arch as its president. In the 1885 General Election he was the first agricultural worker to be elected as a Member of Parliament.

Henry Wright, an employee of William Gascoyne, was two years younger than Joseph Arch and had also grown up in Church Street, Barford. His seventy-eight year old father, Nicholas, was still resident there in 1870, together with his mother and younger brother. On Monday 10th October 1870, Henry Wright was summoned by Mr Stephens, the relieving officer for the Warwick district of the Warwick Union, to appear before magistrates E Dodd and J Moore esquires. He was accused of noncompliance with an order made by the borough magistrates in the previous August. The order had required Henry Wright to contribute 1s. 6d. per week towards the maintenance of his father, a pauper, chargeable to the common fund of the Warwick Union. Henry believed this was an unfair demand for somebody who had served his country as a soldier in the army.

The amount due under the order made by the borough magistrates was 7s. 6d., for five weeks from 22nd August to 26th September 1870. In addition the costs incurred for obtaining the order against the defendant was 13s. 6d. Henry maintained that he only earned about 14 shillings a week, and that when he had paid his rent and other expenses he and his wife had only about 9 shillings to live on. Mr Stephens said he had made enquiries respecting the defendant's means and ascertained that he was employed by Mr Gascoyne, builder, of Leamington. Mr Gascoyne's foreman had informed him, "the defendant was in regular work and earned 18 shillings a week." On this income Henry only had his wife, who took in work at home, to support and her earnings amounted to considerably more than the rent of their cottage, which would be about half-a-crown a week.

In response to the demand, Henry Wright informed the bench he had no intention of paying the money.

Given this response, Mr Moore enquired, "What course of action does the relieving officer want to pursue?"

Mr Stephens replied, "I desire the court to issue a distress warrant for non-payment of the debt." This meant that if payment was not made by the defendant after receiving the distress warrant, then his personal goods could be seized. Mr Moore ordered that the distress warrant be granted.

A defiant Henry Wright then addressed the bench and stated, "I have served eleven years in the army and will go and serve another before I pay 1s 6d. a week out of my small earnings." Henry remained firm and the warrant was enforced against him. He found lodgings and work in Rugby where he remained for a while before eventually returning to Leamington, where he lived in King Street together with his wife, Sarah. Sadly, his father Nicholas died in Barford during October the following year aged seventy-nine.

Occasionally, William reluctantly decided that it was necessary for him to pursue debts through the County Court. In January 1870, he sued Mrs Anna Maria Hobson for £15, for repairs executed to her premises. Mrs Hobson was the widow of Mr Robert Hobson, a former client, for whom William had built Beauchamp Hall in 1864. Unfortunately, Mr Hobson died two years later, leaving Mrs Hobson responsible for the management of the large house. Events had proved difficult for her to manage and although William was sympathetic to her plight, he was not the only creditor in the court on the same day. Leamington butcher Mr Ivan of Warwick Street had taken action to recover £17 outstanding on an account. In both cases the defendant did not appear, and His Honour gave judgement for the plaintiffs and allowed costs in both cases.

On another occasion a disputed repairs bill in October 1883 saw William taking legal action against Mr H B Rathbone, of Portland Street, Leamington. The claim of £12 9s. 6d., was for the outstanding balance of an account for repairs, over two years, to three cottages in Court

Street and Drummond Street, Leamington. The work in dispute was to paint the doors and windows and to put the slates in order. The defendant stated that he ordered £6 or £7 worth of repairs from W. Gascoyne, builder, Leamington, and that the plaintiff sent in a bill for £18. The defendant was asked, "Do you mean to rest your defence upon this, that it was a claim for work not ordered, or that it was an overcharge?"

He responded, "Both." The dispute required a degree of expertise in building and the judgement of the court directed that the question in dispute should be referred to a competent person to decide between the parties. A compromise between the parties was eventually achieved by the arbitrator and a final settlement agreed.

William was not immune to court prosecutions. In June 1881 he had himself appeared before the police court for an Excise prosecution. He was summoned by the Excise for having kept a carriage and also a manservant without a licence. The court supervisor stated Mr Gascoyne had written, explaining that the non-taking out of the licenses was an oversight; the case was adjourned for a fortnight to allow for a settlement. William appreciated the sympathetic judgement of the court and paid the outstanding amount for the licence.

CHAPTER 28

William takes his town house style to the country

The expansion of William's company as a partnership with his sons produced good profits in both Warwickshire and in Kent. William, like many successful contemporary businessmen, aspired to assimilate with the landowning gentry and the family residence became Village Farm, Lillington. William was now overseeing an estate of 286 acres, which incorporated the nearby Manor Farm and employed eleven permanent farmhands. In addition, domestic staff living with the family on the farm included Sarah Allsop, their long-serving family cook. Other residents were Emma Harris, a parlour maid, together with stockman William Harris and his wife Charlotte. The Gascoynes' property in Newbold Road was used solely as an office for their Midland building business.

Although Martha missed the lovely conservatory of the house in Leamington, she was extremely proud of her new home and enjoyed her evenings sitting with William in the garden surrounded by the sounds, sights and smells of Lillington's rural village life. She glowed with pride as she spoke to William. "It seems like only yesterday that we first moved into our little cottage just down the road. We are all so proud of your achievements."

"The boys have played their part," replied William modestly.

"They have an excellent role model in you to follow, and I know our daughters are extremely thankful to their father for the material benefits you have provided for them," said Martha.

Entering the spacious dining room of Village Farm house from the entrance hallway, visitors were struck by the quality of the furnishing, particularly the carved oak chairs and tables. The pleasant, sweet smell from freshly polished surfaces filled the air, and handsome sideboards neatly exhibited an extensive collection of porcelain. Numerous valuable gleaming silver plate and silver-plated goods were proudly displayed. The walls were adorned by an assortment of valuable old oil paintings, engravings and watercolours. A variety of bronze ornaments were strategically placed to complement an excellent example of a fourteen-day timepiece. A musical box provided evidence of the family's enjoyment of music, something that was a particular love of the young Juliet. A bevelled pier glass was flanked by windows. The large mirror was designed to fill the wall space between the windows and during sunny days directed light on to a bold coloured elaborately patterned Turkish carpet.

Next to the dining room, was the parlour, a large, elegant room containing a mahogany suite and dining table. Opposite the doorway sat a functional sideboard displaying high quality tea and dessert services. A handsome pier glass stood proudly against the window wall. The room displayed an impressive collection of marble ornaments and an array of china. An ornate eight-day clock formed an eye-catching focal point for the beautifully decorated room.

The welcoming environs of their drawing room contained walnut furniture including a comfortable upholstered suite together with a set of four carved occasional chairs. A number of tables and an elegant glazed winged cabinet were used to display an impressive collection of antique china together with a silver presentation cup. A circular loo table took a prominent position in the room where members of the family regularly enjoyed playing the card game. In the corner there was a cottage trichord pianoforte which was used to accompany the talented Juliet with her singing. The floor was overlaid with a beautifully made Turkish carpet which complemented a magnificent example of a Japanese lacquered cabinet which stood against the side wall. The highlight of the room was a fireplace with a mantelpiece on which sat a magnificent timepiece accompanied by a pair of vases to match.

From the hall an oak staircase rose to the upper storey where the landing led to six fully furnished well-proportioned bedrooms. Each of the rooms contained beds neatly made up with freshly laundered and pressed bedlinen. The bedrooms were brightly decorated in warm pastel colours and furnished with wardrobes, dressing tables, washstands and mirrors. A selection of landscape paintings, together with a number of family portraits were tastefully positioned in each room. Rugs were placed over the polished oak floorboards in an attempt to reduce the level of impact noise, whilst providing a warm comfortable surface for bare feet.

William was always mindful of providing good sanitary facilities in his family home. His priority after moving to the farm was to connect to the main drainage system and eliminate the use of bucket toilets. In January 1871, William requested the Lillington Local Board of Health to provide a sewer to drain his property in the village. He was informed on this occasion that the owners were responsible for providing drainage to their own properties. William advised the board, "I will provide suitable arrangements for my own property on this occasion, but I will make it my public health mission to ensure that suitable drainage is connected to all properties in the village." He persisted with his campaign until April 1874 when the board requested him to submit plans and estimate for providing a sewer from the Kenilworth Old Road to the village. In order to proceed with the work, the Lillington Local Board borrowed £1,000 on security of the rates, repayable within thirty years, from the Public Works Loan commissioners. William's company eventually laid most of the main sewers in the districts of both Lillington and Milverton.

William undertook his farming venture with his usual desire for achieving the best possible results. His success in farming was recognised before long and celebrated in the local press during Christmas time 1873, when a pig bred by him, which formed the centrepiece of a display by Mr Astell's butcher shop in Warwick Street, was described as, "a perfect beauty in every respect." Christmas was a time when top quality meats of many kinds were demanded for feasting. This required butchers to stock their shops to bursting point at a time when there was no means of preserving their provisions by refrigeration. Their answer to the problem was to hang the meat in a display which completely covered the frontage of their shop. This allowed good ventilation of the goods while allowing the cold winter atmosphere to keep the meat chilled. The butcher shop proprietor and staff used their decorative skills using numerous varieties of birds, including turkey, geese and chicken to produce eye-catching displays which would be admired by their customers. The public recognition of William's quality produce was an accolade he was proud of, and he regarded it as an endorsement of his success in farm management together with respect for his status in the rural community.

CHAPTER 29

William entertains at his son's wedding

The successful establishment of the Gascoyne company's activities in Beckenham encouraged James Gascoyne to set a wedding day to marry a local Leamington girl called Annie Tattersfield. James was twenty-two years old and Annie, who was two years his elder, had developed a friendship during their teenage years in Leamington. Annie had spent time in Beckenham with James while chaperoned by her sister Julia, who was four years her senior. By this time the Gascoyne family had established significant status and influence in Leamington, and any event surrounding the family engendered significant interest amongst the local community.

On Tuesday 24th October 1871, the streets of Lillington village thronged with people estimated to be between two and three thousand in number, who were there to witness the wedding of James and Annie. The bride was the third daughter of Mr Tattersfield, a fishmonger of Bath Street, Leamington, who was a well-known resident of the town. It was announced that the bridal party would walk to the church from the Lillington home of the Gascoyne family. As word of the novel arrangement spread it stimulated tremendous local interest. Those that were most eager to witness the event came early and were crowded into the churchyard and the church. Shortly after eleven o'clock the bridegroom made his way to the church through the rows of spectators that lined the whole of the route.

149

Soon after the bride and the wedding party followed. The bride, who was escorted by her father, was dressed in white silk, with wreath and veil and carried a beautiful bouquet of choice flowers. The bridesmaids comprised two sisters of the bride and three sisters of the bridegroom. All were dressed in dove coloured silks; each also carried a bouquet and they were escorted by the bridegroom's best man, William Gascoyne junior. The procession was headed by James's youngest sister Juliet and his youngest brother Gustave. The wedding guests followed in the rear. These were about a hundred in number consisting of the most intimate friends of the bride and bridegroom's families.

The ceremony at St. Mary Magdalene's parish church was performed by the Rev J Wise, vicar of Lillington, assisted by the Rev W Longhurst, the curate. Given away by her father the bride was the, "cynosure of all eyes", reported the local press. After signing the register the newlyweds drove in carriage and pair back to the Gascoyne residence whilst the rest of the bridal party returned by foot. The pedestrian access to the house from the road was neatly draped and carpeted.

On returning from church the bridal party proceeded to inspect the numerous and beautiful gifts presented to the couple. Standout items amongst the splendid collection included a silver-mounted dressing case, a silver biscuit basket and wine coolers. Prominently displayed were two clocks, one given by the Gascoyne's men at Leamington, and the other by their employees at Beckenham.

The catering for the wedding breakfast was undertaken by Mr Wheal of the Parade, Leamington, and was served in a spacious marquee erected in the garden and furnished for the one hundred guests. An excellent wedding feast was served, followed by toasts and speeches before the cutting of the wedding cake. Shortly after three o'clock the bride and bridegroom departed amid the congratulations and good wishes of their numerous friends, and there followed a shower of old slippers. The couple were driven by horse and carriage to Leamington railway station and left by the 3:55 p.m. train for London, en route to the Isle of Wight for their honeymoon.

During that evening at the Gascoyne's farm in Lillington, a ball took place in the spacious marquee where a boarded floor had been laid down and prepared for dancing to the music of Mr Biggs's quadrille band. An excellent supper was served and about one hundred and forty guests celebrated until an early hour the next morning. Once again William's inclusive instinct towards his employees came to the fore and he used the occasion to show his appreciation of them. The marquee was used on the following evening to serve a celebration dinner provided by William for the men in the firm's employ, together with their wives.

On return from their honeymoon James and his wife established a comfortable family home in Beckenham at 2 Oakhill Villas, Bromley Road, and two years after their marriage they became the proud parents of a healthy son named James William. The following year their daughter Annie Mable was born, and after a lapse of a further two years their second son George Harry was born. William and Martha derived enormous pleasure in their role as grandparents and made visits to see the children whenever possible.

CHAPTER 30

Implications of changing planning laws, materials and institutions

William's attention to farming matters was made possible by the emergence of his older sons' ability to take responsibilities in his building business. The formal creation of the Gascoyne Building Company in 1872 as a trading partnership between William and his sons proved to be a great success. During the following year William believed his various interests were on a sound footing and he could return to public office. He was once again elected to the Leamington Local Board of Health and was appointed to the Committee of Management of the pump rooms and grounds. William again pursued his aim of making the enjoyable amenities of the town available for its residents. Within two years of his return to public office, a resolution was approved by the Local Board for the pump room gardens to be opened to the public free of charge in perpetuity.

In November 1873, when William was chairman of the Highways Committee, he instigated the requirement that all streets in the town should have house numbers with even numbers on the right-hand side and odd numbers on the left side. Each occupier was required to number their house with a number to a pattern provided by the town's surveyor. At this time it was also decided to rename the important thoroughfare in the town where William had his office from Newbold Road to Willes Road. This he declared, "is a reasonable expression of gratitude to

Edward Willes who was one of the most liberal patrons Leamington had known." This gesture was by way of improving the relationship between the town and the Willes family who, as a major landowner, had donated a large portion of their land for recreational purposes to the town. The land had been gratefully received, as its central location along the bank of the River Leam formed an ideal amenity for the residents and visitors to the town. The decision by the town to name the newly landscaped leisure park "the Jephson Gardens", as a tribute to the renowned Doctor Jephson whose national reputation had done much to bring visitors to the spa town, was not met enthusiastically by the Willes family. This attempt to bring the Willes family name to lasting prominence in the town served William favourably in land deals he negotiated with the landowning family.

Legal constraints imposed on the type of building erected on a site, together with control over its subsequent use were controls that continued to be imposed by the time William became a developer. The vendor of a parcel of land often incorporated restrictive covenants in freehold conveyances or restrictive clauses in leasehold transactions. When William Gascoyne purchased freehold land forming Lakelands Meadow from Emily Willes in 1872, it contained a number of conditions that were typical and which appeared in similar contracts for other land deals between the two parties. The only types of building allowed on the site were to be villas or private dwellings worth at least £600 each when completed. Control over which boundaries of the site were to be developed, together with the introduction of a building line of 12 feet, dictated where the houses could be sited and the requirement of a minimum frontage width of 25 feet for each building effectively determined the density of the development. It was also stipulated that the final appearance of the houses was to be to the satisfaction of the vendor or Emily's agent whose approval was required for the elevations of the building to be erected.

At the time strict control was imposed on the builder during the construction of the properties by imposing a ban on the use of clay on the land for making any bricks or tiles and prohibiting the making or burning of any bricks or tiles on the site. The use of the property was restricted in perpetuity by a condition which placed, "a prohibition against any act, matter or thing on any part of the land which should or might be offensive, dangerous or cause nuisance or annoyance to the neighbourhood".

These restrictions dictating the type of property to be built were found particularly onerous during the 1870s when the sale of houses in Leamington became difficult. At this time William had purchased a large parcel of land for residential development on the corner of Binswood Terrace East from the Willes estate, and his subsequent request, "for release from the prohibitive effect of these restrictive covenants," received a favourable response. In order to appeal to a wider range of customers, William resorted to a mixed development for the site, building five expensive detached villas along the frontage to Binswood Terrace with a row of nine terraced houses to the rear along Trinity Street. At each end of the terrace three substantial attached houses faced Clarendon Street and Arlington Avenue.

The initial housing developments by the Gascoyne company were predominantly in the parish of Leamington Priors, but as desirable building plots became scarce he looked to other parishes. In 1875 William was offering to sell four acres of land in the parish of Lillington suitable for one house and a further 13,000 square yards of land in Rugby Road, Lillington, suitable for houses of £1,000 and upwards. By the mid-1870s William and his sons had spread their activities so wide that they could advertise a large quantity of land for sale in Leamington and Beckenham, both on a freehold and leasehold basis, upon which houses could be built to suit any requirements.

Taxation in various forms was a major influence on the number, location and character of houses built. The rating provisions of the Local Improvement Act determined that householders in streets which lacked street lighting or paved footpaths were liable for only two-thirds rates, a situation which encouraged the building of better quality houses on more remote sites which lacked these amenities. The elimination of this anomaly by the implementation of the Public Health Act for Leamington in 1852 had the effect of promoting the trend towards development around the perimeter of the town boundary in neighbouring parishes where the local rates were lower. In November 1870 William Gascoyne applied to the Lillington Local Board of Health for approval to build five houses in Binswood Terrace East, and in 1872 he was requesting permission from the same authority to build on the Rugby Road, a location some distance from the centre of Leamington. By 1878 Gascoyne began to build houses to the Warwick side of the railway track along the Warwick Road, Milverton. The properties in these two parishes did not come under the more onerous rating authority of Leamington until the areas were incorporated into the borough in 1890.

The introduction of new materials together with improvements in existing building materials was influencing both the appearance and the construction of structures. Portland cement, patented by Joseph Aspdin in 1824, brought a revolutionary change in building techniques and was a product readily available to William and Leamington builders from a local primary source, the Rugby Cement Manufacturing Company. Portland cement mixed with sand and aggregate to form concrete became a common substitute for decorative and structural stone as a component in buildings. The use of terracotta was a relatively new decorative material when used by William in 1873 for the ornamental balustrade on the Willes Bridge over the River Leam. The new balustrade for the bridge was designed by local architect John Cundall.

The development of the railway system greatly improved the variety of building materials available to William and other builders in the town. The local building industry was provided with an extended market for the supply of materials from previously uneconomic or inaccessible sources. The slate industry, which had shipped its produce by sea to many parts of Europe, had been given a boost in 1831 when it was decided to repeal the duty on seaborne slate. The repeal of the duty stimulated an era of accelerated growth in the slate industry that was matched by a demand in the home market from the rise in the volume of both residential and industrial construction. Clay roof tiles from local producers became less competitive and were superseded by roof slates sourced from Welsh quarries and brought by steam locomotion trains across the expanding national railway network.

As the network of railways developed, the impact on some Leamington manufacturers and suppliers to the building industry was significant. William's growing business provided a good local customer for the developing Leamington brick producers. In May 1885 the Lillington and Leamington Brick Company had developed a manufacturing capability that allowed it to secure the contract to supply over two million bricks to be used in the National Agricultural Hall (later renamed the Empire Hall, Olympia) on a site adjoining Addison Road Station in Kensington (later renamed Olympia Station). With a total floor area of 110,000 square feet, the hall structure contained the largest area unoccupied by supports of any building in London. The standard size of the Leamington brick was not compatible with the dimensions of bricks used in London. In order to secure the contract in accordance with the client's specification, the Lillington and Leamington Brick Company incurred substantial costs for retooling its production equipment. Unfortunately, friction developed between the two parties to the contract and the agreement for supplying the bricks was terminated prematurely as a result of a legal dispute.

The compulsory provision of plans for approval by local authorities during the second half of the nineteenth century helped to raise and maintain standards. William was enthusiastic to introduce tried and tested good practice in his building company. He was quick to implement standardisation and reused popular and successful house plans for subsequent developments. Soon after introducing a repeated house design for a number of properties built in Newbold Terrace, he used an identical house plan during 1871 for two remote sites in Leamington located in Avenue Road and Binswood Terrace.

Standards in building during the nineteenth century benefited from the establishment of a number of professional bodies whose aim was to improve the knowledge and standard of the construction industry. Pre-eminent amongst the professional organisations were the architects. Although architects' clubs, which were discussion groups for those with mutual interest in architecture, had existed before, it was not until 1834 that the Institute of Architects was formed. The institute was incorporated by Royal Charter in 1837 as the Royal Institute of British Architects. From an early stage in his career William often prepared drawings for his own building work and took responsibility for submitting a client's plans for approval by the local authorities. By the early 1870s his business advertisements described the company as that of "Architects, Surveyors, Builders and Contractors". However, these were titles adopted by William and his sons without any attempt to become chartered architects.

It would seem that Gascoyne's role as an architect was not always a complete success. At a meeting of the Warneford Hospital Committee of Management held on 5th February 1879, the controller read a report advising that the present outpatients department should be converted into a large male accident ward. The proposal was supported by a plan and a report by William showing that the work could be done for £114 19s 0d. On 5th June it was agreed that a sub-committee of three be appointed to consider the proposal, with the power to appoint a professional architect to advise them. It was further ordered that the secretary write to William Gascoyne informing him that the matter would proceed with a professional architect. William was aggrieved by the aspersions cast on his design capabilities and sent a letter dated 16th June complaining about the committee's resolution.

Further doubt about William's design flair was muted at a meeting of the Building Committee of St. Peter Apostle Church, Leamington, held on 29th January 1884. A letter from Reverend Varney Cave outlined his views about improvements that might have been made to the church during reconstruction work on an earlier occasion. In the letter he referred to a design plan for external confessionals he had obtained from the Gascoyne company. The priest stated that, "he had decided against the scheme because the expense was too great," but also because he considered the proposal gave the appearance of a water closet.

CHAPTER 31

Sports development in Leamington

The attraction of Leamington Spa as a health centre produced the need for a supporting set of entertainment and social activities. Apart from pleasure gardens, theatres and gatherings at assembly rooms, sport became an important pastime for many Leamington residents. William believed that promoting sporting activities would lead to improved provisions for public health in the town. Hunting had long been popular in the area and an autumn steeplechase meeting was held annually on Newbold Comyn. In 1829 a Leamington cricket team played on a ground near Newbold Comyn, and around 1850 a cricket club was formed by England players George Parr and John Wisden at Victoria Park. Archery was well established in Leamington by 1833 when an area for it was provided in Newbold Gardens, later known as the Jephson Gardens. In 1852 the "Royal Leamington Archers" held their "First Annual Meeting" on Parr & Wisden's cricket ground. The medieval form of tennis, referred to as "real tennis", was established at the Leamington Tennis Court Club in 1846. William informed his friends and associates, "I have observed that sporting activities often provide healthy purpose-built facilities for the participants and encourage the preservation of healthy large open spaces as playing areas. These all serve as a benefit to the town as a whole. It is my clear intention to promote and support such recreational activities wherever possible."

William eagerly encouraged his family's participation in sporting activities and was supportive of a number of sports clubs. His sons attended the Manor House Academy for their education where they were introduced to a variety of popular sports. The school was housed in the manor house, located on the southern bank of the River Leam in the old town area. The manor house had been built and occupied by the Wise family before they relocated to Shrubland Hall on the outskirts of the town. The Wise family's former house was converted for use as a hotel in 1847 before becoming the Manor House Academy in 1850. After serving as a school for the next twenty years, it became a hotel once again. In 1874 the hotel became the location for the world's first lawn tennis club, "The Leamington Tennis Club", founded in its grounds.

Whilst at the Manor House Academy, William Gascoyne junior acquired a reputation as a talented sportsman and together with his younger brother Gustave represented the academy's cricket team. In 1864, during a local derby match against Brunswick House Academy, the twelve year old William junior was instrumental in achieving a six run victory by taking four wickets in the first innings and six wickets during the second innings. On completion of their schooling, both William junior and Gustave, with the support and encouragement of their father, continued to play the game with the town's cricket club. William became an active member of the Leamington Cricket Club himself and spoke as its chairman during the club's annual dinner held at the Crown Hotel in 1872.

Football in its various forms had long been a popular sport which had been played with no universally defined rules. On 26th October 1863, The Football Association was founded at the Freemasons' Tavern in London and a common set of rules was established which favoured kicking and dribbling with the ball and banned handling except by the goalkeeper. Football clubs that preferred a handling game formed the Rugby Football Union at the Pall Mall Restaurant in London in 1871. Separate codes for association and rugby football now existed and most clubs decided to play one or the other, although some played both codes during the early years of separation. During the decade immediately following the formation of the Rugby Football Union, Midland clubs were formed in Burton, Lutterworth, Moseley, Northampton, Rugby, Coventry, Wolverhampton, Lichfield, Long Buckby, Stratford-upon-Avon, Nuneaton and Leicester. In 1876, the twenty-five year old William Gascoyne junior participated in the founding of a rugby football team in his home town called Leamington Rovers. William junior approached his father to become a sponsor for the club, suggesting that it would raise his profile as a benevolent member of the community.

William was pleased to lend support for healthy activities for his son and others in the town's new sports club. He was acutely aware that an association with the rugby football club was an opportunity for his company to gain greater exposure through the club's fixtures in Leamington and other towns. William arranged to be present on the pitch sideline as the Leamington Rovers played their opening match under rugby union rules against Banbury on Saturday 1st October 1881. It was agreed that home games for the Leamington team would be played at Leam Terrace East and to begin with the club's colours were red and white, although this was soon changed to black with skull and crossbones on the chest.

The physical nature of the game produced a strong dependence on teamwork and comradeship. William junior's substantial body frame and physical strength made him a natural for the sport and he quickly became a regular and popular member of a diverse group of players.

The Rovers team was made up of players from a wide range of backgrounds. A number of them had a college background where they had developed their liking for the game. A doctor and local bank employees together with other business professionals played alongside tradesmen such as the shoemaker brothers Charles and Reuben Standbridge. The brothers had learned their trade from their mother who was a cordwainer in the nearby village of Bubbenhall. Teddy Ivens, a baker from Shipston-on-Stour, regularly travelled a considerable distance along the Fosse Way in order to play. William junior, a stout, hard playing forward became a well-established member of the club and on occasions recruited other family members to play for the team. Because of the nature of his family's building business, William junior was popularly known as "Bodger" by his fellow team members.

CHAPTER 32

Building trade disputes

The agreement made between the Leamington building employers and bricklayers in 1870 ran its full course. In January 1873 the representatives of bricklayers, masons, plasterers, carpenter and joiners, plumbers and painters of the trade societies of Leamington grouped together to form the Leamington Trades Council in order to compile a set of rules which they presented to the Leamington builders. Their demands included a reduction in working hours, an increase in rates of pay and improved working conditions. This was the first time that there was combined action by the different building trades in Leamington in order to obtain an overall working agreement for the industry. William perceived this action as the defining moment of significant change in labour relations within the Leamington construction industry.

A well-attended meeting of builders and employers in every branch of the building trade was held at the pump rooms on Thursday 23rd January 1873, to consider the new rules presented by the trade council and to consider the advisability of forming an association of masters, to secure unanimity and concerted action amongst employers of labour. The unanimous consensus of the meeting was that it was impossible to accede to the demands of the men and also that an association should be formed. The title adopted by the group was "The Central Association of Master Builders" and William Gascoyne was appointed the president.

The structure of negotiations within the local building industry had now developed into a sophisticated system involving the industry as a whole and was greatly influenced by the regional and national perspective. The establishment of two broadly-based organisations with a strong commitment to promoting the interests of their respective members provided a catalyst for conflict in the industry locally. William now saw his role as the lead partner in a business with his sons rather than a sole trader and predominantly a champion of his family interests. It was at this point he decided that his loyalties would be with the members of his family together with the employers and his empathy with the operatives diminished.

William, acting on behalf of the building employers, informed the operatives that the employers would not accede to the demands being made and stated, "The present conditions of the building trade, coupled with the increased cost of all kinds of materials, rendered it impossible to grant either shorter hours or increased pay." He set out the employers' proposition that, "The hour rate of wages will remain the same, no constraints would be placed on the employer in his choice of employees or their number and no master nor men will discriminate against a man of membership or non-membership of a society. All trade disputes will be settled by six members of the association together with six members from the trade in dispute, with an umpire to make a binding and conclusive decision on any undecided matters. These rules will apply for a period of two years commencing on 31st March 1873."

A meeting of nearly five hundred building operatives chaired by John Michael, a journeyman carpenter, was held in the public hall, Windsor Street, on Tuesday 11th March 1873. A resolution was adopted by the meeting, "to approach the employers and propose that all matters in dispute should be referred to a board of arbitration." The following day a letter to this effect was sent to Mr Thomas Mill, the secretary of the Builders' Association. A letter of response from the employers took exception to what was claimed to be, "unjust statements made by the chairman during the operatives' meeting". It demanded that the aspersion cast by John Michael should be withdrawn and asserted that, "there would be no more correspondence until that time". This was a stance endorsed by William. In a letter, dated 19th March 1873, to the *Leamington Courier*, John Michael suggested that Mills had, "unduly sensitive feelings and denied having made any untrue or unjust statements". This intransigence displayed by both parties was a signal that a point of conflict had come.

On 21st March 1873, the bricklayers, together with the masons, carpenters and plasterers, were given the sanction of their respective societies to strike if need be. Ten days later the operatives began their strike, an action which was complete throughout the trades except for a small number of painters. Even the non-society men had made common cause with the society men. In anticipation of an action, the masters had cleared up pressing work outstanding and had declined to take on fresh projects until the strike was over. The local press on 3rd April 1873 reported, "both sides appeared to have prepared for a conflict between capital and labour, the like of which has not occurred in Leamington". A consequence of this type of action by the workforce and the response of the employers by withholding their entrepreneurial input had been accurately predicted by William in a letter to the press some twelve years earlier. A week later William's perception proved profound as the newspaper reported, "A number of carpenters, joiners, and labourers had left Leamington for work elsewhere, their fares being paid by various unions".

On Thursday 24th April 1873, William presided over a large attendance of the Leamington Builders' Association at the pump rooms to consider two letters received from the Leamington Trades Council, renewing their desire for arbitration. A resolution was passed stating that the association should adhere to the rules and regulations it had previously issued. However, at this time there were obvious signs of weakness developing on behalf of both parties to the dispute. It was revealed at the meeting that at least one of the association's members had acceded to the operatives' demands. It was further stated that nearly a quarter of the operatives were now back at work. During the following week another letter from the trade council was sent to the Builders' Association asking for a meeting to settle the dispute, but once again the request was rejected.

The continued intransigence of the Builders' Association led to further divisions between its members, culminating in the decision of Mr Bradshaw, the vice-president, to withdraw from the group. Bradshaw along with seven other builders met with the operatives and agreed upon a set of working rules and a wage rate of 6½d. per hour. On 9th August 1873, the General Secretary of the Operative Bricklayers' Society paid the Leamington men their strike pay for the last time. The gross cost of the strike for that particular union had been £323 7s. 3d. The strike of 1873 had lasted for nineteen weeks and the outcome had finished with William still adhering to his argument that the market did not allow for concessions to be made to the Leamington workers. By this time a thriving branch of his business had been established in Beckenham, Kent, and he, unlike his fellow Leamington town builders, was not reliant solely on his Leamington-based business.

William was aware that the loss of wages during the industrial dispute produced ongoing financial pressure for many of the tradesmen. One high profile case in particular caught the attention of people in the Leamington area. On Christmas Day 1874, Alfred Crisp, the Leamington secretary of the Operative Stone Masons' Friendly Society, received a £5 note from the central committee secretary. The money had been granted to the Leamington branch by the central committee to buy hospital tickets for the use of its members requiring medical attention. This access to funds served as too much of a temptation for Crisp who was in financial difficulties due to his loss of earnings during the period of industrial unrest in the construction industry. Having issued an official receipt for the money, he then, without paying the hospital fee as was intended, entered the sum of £4 4s. 0d. in the quarterly account sheet as a subscription paid to the Warneford Hospital.

Crisp's action was brought to light by Stephen Stroud, who was the treasurer of the Lodge, when he asked Crisp for the hospital tickets.

Crisp told him, "The hospital has not printed the tickets and will not do so until the end of January."

Feeling uncomfortable with the response received, Stephen Stroud continued, "In that case would you let me have the hospital receipt for the £4 4s 0d?"

Crisp made the excuse that, "I left it at home in another jacket and will bring it along to the next Lodge night." Unhappy with the situation Stroud decided to delve deeper, and on discovering a signature forged on the quarterly account he questioned the secretary of the hospital who informed him the hospital tickets had been printed in December 1874 and had been ready for distribution on 1st January 1875. With the information gathered, Stroud decided to report the incident to the appropriate authorities.

Crisp was apprehended and committed by the magistrates to take his trial at Warwick Assizes. The first witness called by Crisp at his trial was Brother Frederick Orman, who stated that, "I recollect hearing it said in June and July 1874 that Crisp was to retain the money in his possession and not take out any tickets from the hospital until they were wanted." He further stated that, "There has been no Lodge meeting to order Crisp to pay the money." He maintained that this was because member numbers available to attend meetings were so few that they did not constitute a Lodge.

Similar supportive evidence for Crisp was given by fellow Lodge member James Laite who maintained that, "Unless six members were present it was not a Lodge meeting and that no business could be done." Since no such number had attended at Leamington since Crisp had received the money, he could not be ordered to hand over the money to the hospital.

Brother Timothy Smith, also appearing for Crisp, added that, "the Lodge had approved money for Crisp to recompense him for losses he had sustained through taking a prominent part in the late dispute in Leamington."

The jury at his trial returned a verdict of not guilty for Crisp who avoided punishment by the court. However, this was not an acceptable conclusion for the Operative Stone Masons' Friendly Society. They believed that intimidation and collusion between Crisp and his three supportive trial witnesses had brought about a miscarriage of justice. As a result the four members were expelled from the society. The expulsion remained in place for two years until the Leamington Lodge became acutely aware that their position in industrial negotiations could be undermined by non-member tradesmen being available to employers. In August 1877 an appeal by the members of Leamington Lodge to the central council to reinstate Orman, Laite and Smith was upheld.

CHAPTER 33

Changes in the Gascoyne Building Company
as the family move on

William's reputation as a proactive champion for advancements in Leamington Spa and promoting its image meant that his involvement was often sought for community matters. In October 1872, a public meeting was convened at the town hall in the High Street, Leamington, by the Chairman of the Local Board to promote an application by the town for a Charter of Incorporation. William was selected at the meeting to serve on the committee established to progress the application, which resulted in a charter being granted in February 1875. He attended the final meeting of the Local Board of Health for the District of Leamington which was held at the town hall on Tuesday 6th June 1875. He stood as a successful candidate for the inaugural Leamington Town Council, receiving three hundred and seventy-eight votes, in the West Ward of the first council elections held on 10th July 1875. During the first meeting of the Town Council of Royal Leamington Spa held at the town hall on Monday 12th July 1875, he was elected as an alderman. At the town council meeting held on 26th July he was appointed to serve as a member of the Finance Committee, the Highways, Waterworks, Improvements and Sewerage Committee and the Public Purposes Committee. He was appointed chairman of the latter committee at a meeting on 13th September the same year.

On 10th April 1876, William was appointed to a five-man sub-committee to consider the most suitable site for the erection of a new town hall. However, due to pressure of his business commitments, William submitted a letter of resignation dated 7th October to the council meeting held on 9th October 1876. In his letter to the mayor and members of the town council, he made a request, "to be allowed to resign my seat as I am unable to attend to the duties, owing to my time being fully occupied in my business." He contended, "I am quite unwilling to hold an appointment to which I cannot give my proper attention. By so doing I am deceiving the burgesses of the ward who placed me there and was also keeping out someone who, no doubt, could give the necessary time to it." He further stated, "I have served the town for about ten years and should like now be allowed to retire, at least for a time." William advised the council, "I delayed asking this until the forthcoming general election, hoping to prevent the necessity of two elections which would have taken place had I resigned before."

Alderman Bright proposed that the resignation of Alderman Gascoyne, "Be accepted on payment of the sum of £25, the price accorded under the by-laws in such cases."

The mayor then said, "If the fine was paid on the following morning there would be just time to take the necessary steps for the election of three members instead of two for the West Ward." The proposition was carried unanimously.

Although business in Warwickshire was proceeding satisfactorily, the Gascoyne Building Company affairs in Beckenham were not going as well as William had anticipated. James proved not to possess his father's drive or business acumen and often neglected his duties. Much of his time was spent socialising in the local ale houses and his relationship with Annie started to deteriorate. His

172

disinterest in the success of the business resulted in concern and condemnation from his father. On 20th December 1877 the business partnership was dissolved, and during the following January company advertisements in the local press omitted his sons from the company title. James was removed from the family business by mutual consent and attempts were made to protect some of the family's property from William's liabilities.

The neglect shown towards his family led Annie and James to separate in 1879. Annie returned to Leamington with her three children and set up home at The Manse, Mill Street. In order to support herself and her family she commenced employment as a schoolmistress. James had now lost his family and his business reputation was in tatters.

Despite James's activities in Kent causing William a period of uncertainty, the Gascoyne family were able to celebrate a happy occasion on 17th August 1881 when William junior married Annie Maude Knight at Leamington All Saints parish church. William declared, "Under no circumstances is the behaviour of James to impact on the events for the happy couple." William junior had proved to be an able assistant and was responsible for designing a number of the Gascoynes' building projects; accordingly, he recorded his occupation in the wedding register as an architect. The estranged relations James had with his family led him to miss his brother's wedding. In the absence of James, the couple's entry in the wedding register was witnessed by the groom's siblings Annie and Gustave.

The non-attendance of James at William junior's wedding meant that he thought it too embarrassing for him to face his family at his sister Martha's wedding. On 10th May 1882 William's third daughter, Martha, affectionately known as "Mattie", married Richard Walmesley. The wedding took place at St. Peter Apostle Roman Catholic Church, Leamington, the building her father had constructed twenty years previously. William was happy to see the couple's union and used his connections with local dignitaries of the Catholic Church to help with proceedings. The service was conducted by the Rev J J Verres, of Baddesley Clinton for whom the Gascoyne family business had recently successfully designed and completed a new presbytery. The celebrant was assisted during the service by the Rev Father Kelly, of Warwick.

Richard Walmesley's family home was Pilgrims Hall, Brentwood, Essex, and he had attended the prestigious Roman Catholic boarding school Stonyhurst College in Lancashire during the 1860s. (This college was attended soon after by Arthur Conan Doyle, the writer who achieved fame for his detective fiction featuring the character Sherlock Holmes.) On leaving college Richard decided to enter the brewing industry. Richard and Martha settled in Bradford, Yorkshire, and had three sons between 1883 and 1889. In 1890 the family moved to Cheshire where their two daughters were born. Their eldest son, Bernard, emigrated to Canada in 1901, and he was joined by his brothers Cuthbert in 1907 and Oswald in 1908. In 1910 Richard and Martha, together with their daughters Monica and Winifreda joined their sons in Canada.

During his time in Beckenham James Gascoyne was enthralled by stories his drinking companions told about the wealth discovered by opportunists in the gold fields of Australia. He felt the desperate need to get away to begin a new life and decided that a bold move of this type might be his best option. Early in 1882 James travelled to Liverpool and made his way to the docks area. As nightfall arrived, he went down to the quays and for a while stood close to the edge and stared into the murky water. He pondered what it would be like if he were to jump in and put an end to his misery. For a moment it seemed like it could be the answer to everything that was wrong in his life. All of a sudden he felt the cold of the night air and it brought him abruptly to his senses. He eventually made his way towards the *Macbeth*, a cargo vessel out of Glasgow that was to set sail for Australia on 7th February. James was one of fourteen passengers who were prepared to endure the cramped conditions aboard the ship for a journey lasting three months.

The *Macbeth* docked at Melbourne, Victoria, on 8th May 1882. Once disembarked, James made his way by train to the Melbourne terminus on Flinders Street, in the centre of the city. The station consisted of a long platform, partially covered with an overhanging sun canopy supported off timber weatherboard clad buildings. As he exited on to the bustling street he had a feeling of adventure and excitement. James wandered into the first bar that he came to in the hope of engaging with someone who could assist him to find a job that would help to fund his prospecting ambition. To his dismay he found that the rewards of the gold rush had already peaked and the prospect of making a fortune in the Victoria gold fields was all but over. It would be a long time before any news of James would reach his family back in England.

CHAPTER 34

Contracts with the Catholic Church

William was intent on resolving his business difficulties by making a concerted effort, with the support of William junior, to profit from his building activities in the Midlands. On 1st May 1877, Canon Jeffries agreed that the Gascoyne company would erect a 220 feet tower and spire at St. Peter Apostle Church at a cost of £3,000, with a completion date of 1st December in the same year. At this time William's extended business activity was beginning to show evidence of strain on his company's finances. Company cashflow issues resulted in William applying for an early payment of £500 for work in connection with the building of the new campanile. Canon Jeffries reported that William had been in direct contact with the Church's bank and had received notice that the bank was prepared to pay him the money owed for the contract without the two weeks request notice. The bank paid interest on a half yearly basis for the Church's funds deposited with them and the withdrawal of money at the time William required it would mean the loss of some interest. William's need for funds at this time was such that he indicated that he was prepared to reimburse the Church for any loss of interest incurred. The payment which had been approved by an architect's certificate from the architect Mr Clutton was sanctioned by Canon Jeffries to proceed on this basis. The building contract for the tower was successfully completed and the bells were placed within and blessed during November 1878.

Signs of William's possible financial difficulties had little impact on his working relationship with the Roman Catholic Church at this time. During the following year the Gascoyne Building Company submitted the successful competitive tender of £1,240 to the architect Mr J R Donnelly, of Coventry to build the Roman Catholic schools in Leamington. The schools were erected near the existing convent in Augusta Place as a consequence of the government inspectors' report that the existing accommodation was insufficient for the number of girls and infants educated by the nuns.

The Gascoyne's building work for Roman Catholic schools continued during 1880 when the convent school and orphanage in the nearby Warwickshire market town of Southam were found to be inadequate. In Southam a German order of nuns provided the care for orphan girls and the education of children in general. The new building was erected by the Gascoyne company in accordance with plans prepared by William Gascoyne junior. Built in red brick and measuring about 70 feet by 30 feet, it was situated upon the ground attached to the convent on the road to Daventry and commanding a fine view of the surrounding country. The ground floor consisted of a large schoolroom running the whole length of the building, divided by a wooden screen so as to form two classrooms, one for the boys and the other for the girls. The second floor served as a girl's dormitory, about 50 feet by 25 feet, and the top floor was divided into two rooms, to serve as sick wards. The building cost of £1,400 was defrayed in part by the community of the convent and in part by friends and benefactors sympathising with the work to which the sisters had devoted themselves.

William was curious about the presence of nuns in Southam at this time and he was fascinated as the parish priest informed him how it owed much to earlier events in Europe. "The post-Napoleonic period had witnessed the demise of the Holy Roman Empire, which created new dynamics in the political powers of Europe. In 1861 William I became Prussian King and appointed Otto von Bismarck as Chief Minister. During this time Prussia became a leading player in the attempt to create a confederation of German states. Victory in the Franco-Prussian War during 1870–71 presented an opportunity for Bismarck to achieve a unified Germany. Roman Catholics now represented thirty per cent of the new state's population. In 1870, the First Vatican Council declared the dogma of papal infallibility and there was now a perceived conflict of divided loyalty between the State and the Church. Bismarck pursued a cultural struggle with Catholics in Germany by legislation restricting the Catholic Church's political power. All of the Church's schools were placed under state control and the Jesuits were expelled."

"But how did it result in the nuns being in England?" William asked eagerly seeking more information.

"The conflict between the emerging German nation state and the Catholic Church had resulted in the 'Sisters of the Poor Child Jesus' being exiled by the Bismarck Laws from Germany. The nuns sought refuge in England, establishing a house in Southam in 1876 and they opened an orphanage soon after. They brought with them the German method of teaching which was regarded by the education authorities to be one of the best public methods of instruction."

"Is that a fact?" questioned William.

"Evidence suggested it to be true," said the priest. "During an examination by Her Majesty's Inspectors in

July 1880, the elementary schools in Oxford, taught by other members of this community, recorded a ninety-nine per cent pass rate for their pupils."

"A very impressive achievement," William responded, and then thanked the priest for his very informative explanation.

William Gascoyne junior's design skills were employed once more for a Catholic Church building during the following year. In the summer of 1881, a new presbytery, at a cost in excess of £700, was in the course of erection by the Gascoyne company at Baddesley Clinton, Warwickshire. A fundraising event for the new building, in the form of a fancy fair, was held on Tuesday 12th and Wednesday 13th July in the stunning grounds of Baddesley Clinton Hall. The event took place in a tent erected for the purpose on the front lawn and the exhibits were displayed on stalls.

Contributions to the various stalls had been donated from a wide variety of sources. Locally Mr Burman gave a gold watch and several electro-plated articles, while Mrs Rosa Muller of Bristol sent two charming watercolour drawings. On one stall there was an extensive display of beautiful embroidery created by the Southam nuns. Another stall was wholly devoted to a splendid display of locally sourced top quality fruit and flowers. Paintings on porcelain and terracotta that had been skilfully executed by Miss Monica Drinkwater proved to be very popular. Among the curiosities were sets of cups made of wood from the thousand year old boundary oak tree of the parishes Baddesley Clinton and Temple Balsall. Of particular interest to William was a fine oil painting exhibited on one of the stalls prior to being auctioned. Valued at 100 guineas, the painting was generously presented by Mr E H Dering. The refreshment department, serving cakes and cold drinks, was entrusted to Mr and Miss Clara Brunner of Birmingham.

The medieval moated manor house of Baddesley Clinton dated from the fifteenth century and had been the home to the Ferrers family for five hundred years. The family had long connections with the Catholic Church and the manor house contained a number of priest holes from earlier times. Members of the Jesuit missionary group were believed to have held meetings there, including Henry Garnett the English Jesuit leader executed for his complicity in the Gunpowder Plot of 1605. William walked along the stone bridge over the water-filled moat leading to the main entrance to the building. He lingered for a while and spent some time appreciating the craftsmanship of the structure and empathising with the medieval stonemasons who had been responsible for the magnificent facade. William pondered the historical events that may have been witnessed within the walls of the building. Although during his lifetime there were still some areas of resistance to the Roman Catholic Church's advancement in England, William reflected on how his involvement with the Church could have made him and his family so vulnerable only a couple of centuries earlier.

As William joined the fashionable and influential attendees on each of the two days, he was fully aware of the public relations and marketing opportunity for his building business that the Baddesley Clinton event presented. He entered into polite conversation as he intermingled among the distinguished socialites such as Lady Cartwright, Mrs Willes, and Mrs A Newdigate. William used the opportunity to network with prominent members of the Roman Catholic clergy in attendance, including The Rev Canon Longman, Vicar General. The incumbent Baddesley Clinton parish priest, the Rev Verres, was happy to introduce William to representatives from other parishes in the Roman Catholic diocese including, Hampton-on-the-Hill, Birmingham, Husbands Bosworth, Selly Oak, Warwick, and Kenilworth. By way of promoting of the Gascoyne building company, it was announced during the course of the fundraising event that the work on the new presbytery had been in hand three weeks and already good progress was being made.

The Roman Catholic Church had been a regular source of business for the Gascoyne company and William was keen to establish new contacts within the Church at this time. The happy working relationship that Gascoyne had enjoyed with Canon Jefferies had come to an end with the death of the canon in January 1880. This sad loss happened at a time when William felt the need of support from long established friends in business. This was later compounded when the symbol of the two men's working relationship, St. Peter Apostle Church, was badly damaged by fire on 11th November 1883, as a result of carelessness with a lighted candle by a person employed to tune the church organ.

The Gascoyne Building Company was instructed by the Church Building Committee of St. Peter Apostle Church to do the initial repair work and prepare a valuation for the insurance claim for which William received a fee of £89 4s 5p. The initial estimate of rebuilding the church was put at £4,500, of which only £2,249 18s 4d was covered by insurance. It was decided that the balance was to be raised by voluntary contributions. At a meeting on 10th January 1884, the building committee discussed the possibility of awarding the work to Gascoyne as a negotiated contract. However, concerns were raised about rumours circulating about how the Gascoynes were suffering difficulties with their business activities. William no longer had Canon Jefferies to champion his cause and the members of the Church Building Committee were more reticent about awarding him the contract.

The committee instructed their agent Mr Cox to prepare plans, specification and quantities to be sent to selected contractors for competitive tender. William Gascoyne submitted the lowest tender of £1,750 which was accepted by the building committee on 28th February, subject to approval of the architect. At a subsequent meeting of the committee on 2nd March 1884, it was decided that the contract should be awarded to George F Smith of Milverton, who had submitted an amended tender price of £1,496. It was further agreed that William would be paid for the work already done as soon as possible. Gascoyne's account, however, was only settled after a dispute regarding the amount of his charges. It was claimed that a charge of £25 for making the valuation for the insurance claim was excessive. This episode marked the demise of the association between Gascoyne and the Roman Catholic Church in Leamington.

CHAPTER 35

The effects of bankruptcy

Six years after dissolving the business partnership with his sons, William believed he had got his business affairs under control. During 1883 he was encouraged by fellow town residents to stand once again as a candidate in the annual elections for the town council. On 1st November 1883 he was elected for the North West Ward, and at a meeting of the council the following week he was appointed to the Highways, Waterworks, Improvements and Sewerage Committee and as a member of the Committee of Management of the pump room. There was further recognition of his highly regarded knowledge and expertise on 10th December 1883 when he was appointed as one of seven members of the council to form a special Municipal Building Committee. The brief of the committee was to oversee the building of the new town hall, and it was recommended that they should send a deputation to visit the Council House in Birmingham to ascertain the mode of furnishing for the council chamber and committee rooms. On 11th February 1884, a list of suitable furnishings was presented by the committee to the council meeting for consideration.

William continued with his desire to promote the town's facilities for its residents. He was keen that access to knowledge should be made available to all that sought it. He took a great interest in the growth of the free library and made every endeavour as a councillor to get it properly housed. At a meeting of the council held on 15th

April 1884, William moved that seven rooms under the ballroom at the new municipal building, be let to the Free Library Committee for the purpose of a free library. The Municipal Buildings were opened on 18th September 1884, and on 8th December of that year the offer to provide accommodation for the free library was accepted. It was to remain the home for the library until a purpose-built free library building was eventually erected in 1900.

William's efforts to revive his flagging business were not going to plan and he reluctantly accepted that his position was becoming increasingly untenable. As a man of honour, he realised it was his civic duty to withdraw from public office. His letter of resignation from the town council for a second time was submitted on 17th January 1885. On this occasion the resignation was accepted by the council without the imposition of any fine. It was recorded by Alderman Harding that the council was losing, "the practical and valuable service of Mr Gascoyne".

The date of William's letter of resignation from the council was significant, for on 17th December 1884 a Receiving Order under the Bankruptcy Act 1883 was made against him at the County Court of Surrey at Croydon. The local Leamington press reported that he had been compelled to file a partition in bankruptcy and therefore vacate his seat. It suggested that this was a situation to be regretted, "not only on account of Mr Gascoyne who as an old and respected resident deserves the sympathy of all classes, but also in the interests of the town", and contended that, "his special business qualifications and local experience rendered his presence in the council particularly desirable".

At a sitting of the Warwick County Court during January 1885, William was also being sued by the London and North Western Railway Company to cover £21 4s 10d., alleged to be due for carriage. However, Mr Burr, on behalf of the railway company, applied for an adjournment on account of the partition filed by another creditor against William in bankruptcy No.33 of 1884. At the Surrey County Court, a Receiving Order was made on 7th December 1884 and the first meeting of creditors was ordered for 26th January. The date set by the Croydon court for the public examination of the debtor was 30th January 1885.

The origin of William's financial problems had stemmed from the activities in Beckenham of his son James who had unfortunately let him into some heavy liabilities. William had ownership of a large estate in Beckenham which had depreciated in value, and as soon as he had realised he could not obtain any further advance on his property he called together a meeting of creditors. An offer of 5 shillings in the pound was made and a great number of creditors were in favour of acceptance, but it was opposed by the Official Receiver who wanted 6 shillings in the pound. At a meeting of the creditors held at Croydon on Monday 2nd February 1885, it was resolved to accept a composition of 6s. 8d. in the pound, payable as 5s. in the pound in one month, and 1s. 8d. in the pound in seven months from the date of approval by the court.

The Official Receiver, Cecil Mercer, gave notice that William Gascoyne, Builder and Contractor of Beckenham, Kent, Leamington and Lillington, both in Warwickshire, was on 10th April 1885 adjudged bankrupt by the County Court of Surrey. Six days later Ernest Forman, an

185

accountant and secretary to the Timber Trade Association, of 57 Gracechurch Street, London, was duly appointed and certified by the Board of Trade as trustee.

Mr Forman, the trustee, issued an official proclamation in the press stating, "All persons having in their possession any of the effects of the bankrupt must deliver them to me and all debts due to the bankrupt must be paid to me. Creditors who have not yet proved their debts must forward their proofs of debts to me".

On 9th June 1885, Mr E Hazle, auctioneer, of 114 Victoria Street, London, by order of the trustee in bankruptcy, offered for sale the household furniture, farm stock, crops and farm implements upon the premises of "The Farm", Lillington, belonging to William Gascoyne. The inventory prepared for the sale included an extensive array of mahogany and oak furniture, Turkish carpets, oil paintings, four-wheeled carriages and horse saddles. The range and quality of the items offered in the sale reflected the property of a man of substance and wealth.

The financial difficulties experienced by the company impacted not only the employees and creditors of the company, but also the fortunes of Leamington institutions supported by the Gascoyne family. Although Leamington Rovers Football Club had achieved a substantial membership, it had suffered from the perennial problem of collecting subscriptions. The Gascoyne family business had maintained a close connection with the club through the continuous playing membership of William junior, and the company had been a benefactor throughout the club's existence. The unfortunate affairs of the Gascoyne Building Company had a direct impact on the financial support it offered to the club, and by 1885 the club was saddled with substantial liabilities. The lack of sponsorship from William's company led significantly to the imminent demise of the football club.

CHAPTER 36

Bankruptcy proceedings

William continued with a forlorn hope that he would be able to salvage some semblance of his reputation and make good his debts by completion of a contract he had undertaken for the construction of a new Salvation Army barracks in Park Street, Leamington Spa. The cost of the project was largely defrayed out of a bequest of £3,700 left by Miss Harvey for the purpose. The freehold site acquired for the new building cost £1,730 and was occupied by the Royal Oak, an ale house of some public repute. William's estimate for the building, including seating and lighting, of about £2,000 was accepted after competitive tendering had taken place. The new building was a typical late nineteenth century citadel constructed in red brick with battlemented towers flanking a three-storey elevation. Designed by the Salvation Army's architect, Mr E J Sherwood of London, it provided accommodation for some two thousand people.

The official opening of the completed building by the army's founder, General William Booth, was programmed for Thursday 23rd June 1885. On Wednesday, the day before the opening, a rumour spread in the town that bailiffs had been put in possession of the building, seizing not only the fittings but also the provisions stored there for the celebration tea to follow the opening ceremony. In addition, they had refused to admit the Salvation Army's officers until money due to the builder, reputed to be £1,800, was paid.

A local Salvationist, Captain Archer, travelled to London to report the matter to his superior and returned the following morning with a cheque for £600 which was paid to the representative of the trustee of the Gascoyne estate. However, the army was still refused possession of the building, and as details of the affair spread a large crowd gathered to watch the proceedings. There followed a period of negotiations between Captain Archer and the representative of the trustee, before the army was eventually allowed to have the key on the promise that the balance of the money due should be paid within a week and if not the keys would be returned.

The extent of William's financial problems was now becoming very clear. At a meeting of Lillington Local Board of Health held on Monday 7th December 1885, the clerk read a letter from the Board of Trade with respect to rates due from the estate of William Gascoyne senior. It stated that, "assuming the accuracy of the trustee's account, there was not likely to be anything available for the creditors, either preferential or otherwise". It advised that, "the trustee had carried out a large contract in Leamington on which the debtor was engaged, in connection with which there had been a heavy loss". At a subsequent meeting of the Lillington Board held on 4th January 1886, the clerk was instructed to take proceedings against the trustee to recover the amount of the rates due to the board from the debtor.

The continuing respect for William was expressed in the sympathy shown for him from his former business associates. During the following month at the Croydon County Court before Judge Lushington, an application was made for the discharge of William Gascoyne. Mr H F Dickens, instructed by Messrs A Hammond, solicitors, of

189

41 Bedford Row, London, supported the application together with a large number of creditors. William's assets had been estimated at £1,699 and unsecured liabilities were £5,600, however, the Official Receiver stated that assets actually realised £1,890. Despite this fact, Mr Dickens reported, "Since the notice of the bankruptcy, the whole of the assets have been swallowed up in a Salvation Army contract at Leamington which had been carried out by the trustee, Mr Foreman."

The Croydon Court was informed, "The trustee had been advised by Gascoyne that the citadel contract would make a great profit and would cost only approximately £500 to complete it. This assessment had proved misguided and the final cost to finish the project was in excess of £1,100." The Official Receiver did not attribute any fraud or any other motive on the part of the bankrupt in the information he gave to the trustee, but only negligence. The Official Receiver, however, opposed the application for discharge. "The books of the bankrupt were not kept in a satisfactory manner and from them it was not possible to ascertain his standing before the bankruptcy." His criticism of William's trading practice continued. "Gascoyne's secured liabilities were not shown, which are the most important things for a builder to show."

The judge in his summing up alluded to the magnitude of William's undertakings and the fact that in common with many other builders he had mortgaged his estate up to the hilt, and like a great number of others in his line of business it had resulted in financial disaster. However, he contended, "The fact that the bankrupt has not kept proper books was the main consideration in coming to this decision." He continued with a condescending tone in his voice. "The bankrupt belonged to a class who were wasting money and destroying the credit of the country for good faith and good honour." On 16th February 1886, William Gascoyne's application for discharge was refused. William was distraught by the news but was magnanimous in defeat and expressed his heartfelt thanks to all who had faith in his intentions and stood by him at this difficult time.

CHAPTER 37

Further Gascoyne bankruptcy

During the turmoil surrounding William's bankruptcy proceedings, William Gascoyne junior was always a loyal support for his father in business. In an attempt to preserve his own career, and in the hope that he might salvage the reputation of his family, William junior in November 1884 started advertising his services in the Leamington press as an architect and surveyor operating from the original family home and company premises at Willes Road, Leamington. In anticipation of forthcoming proceedings against his father and his building company, arrangements had been made so that the Willes Road property would not form part of William's estate for the purpose of any bankruptcy settlement.

William junior decided that his years of experience working with his father's family building company had equipped him with the knowledge and skills he needed in order to establish a similar business of his own. William junior and his wife occupied the Willes Road house together with William's younger brother Gustave who acted as his building manager. William junior had capital of £10 but knew that by association with his father he would be inhibited by a damaged business reputation. As a gesture of goodwill and as an attempt at damage limitation, he accepted liability of £400 for his father's business affairs, which he anticipated paying out of the profit he expected to make from his new business.

During 1885 William junior undertook a variety of building contracts and his new venture showed sound promise during the following four years while producing a reasonable income. He traded from the Leamington property with a business operating on a smaller scale compared with that of his father's former company. The new firm's building stock and equipment could be easily accommodated in the coach house and stable area fronting Cross Street at the rear of the Willes Road house. William junior employed fewer men and the adjacent builder's workshop and yard were largely unused and deserted.

William junior decided to develop the surplus former workshops and associated land assets into cash to help fund further projects. In June 1889 planning permission was granted for the construction of six cottages along Cross Street, Leamington, on the site of the company's workshops. In September 1890 William junior sold two cottages he had built and had successfully let to permanent tenants in Guy Street, Leamington. These were the last developments in the town of Royal Leamington Spa by members of the Gascoyne family.

The successful completion of these profitable developments encouraged thoughts of further speculative schemes. With this intention in mind, William junior looked to the Warwickshire settlement of Birmingham where development land was available at a more advantageous price. Commerce and industry, combined with good transport links, made Birmingham the fastest growing urban centre with the second largest population in England during the nineteenth century. The clearance of slums and the regeneration of parts of the city centre introduced by the mayor Joseph Chamberlain, together with his Liberal colleagues, was perceived by many other city authorities as the ideal model for good municipal government. In recognition of its growing importance, Birmingham was granted city status by Queen Victoria in 1889.

William junior obtained finance through land mortgages to purchase his building plots. In 1891 as more finance was required, he began to borrow money from loan offices at very expensive repayment rates of upwards of forty per cent. This allowed him to start work on twenty-eight houses at Balsall Heath, an area near to the centre of Birmingham. During 1891, in order to satisfy its increasing need for development land, the boundaries of Birmingham had been extended to incorporate Balsall Heath, together with Harborne, Saltley and Ward End. It was William junior's intention to obtain sales for the properties to finance the work as it proceeded. However, sales did not materialise as hoped and he had to resort to borrowing additional money from several friends. This new source of funding allowed him to proceed with the development of nine of the properties.

William junior had kept a daybook but not a cost book, though the latter was a necessary requirement of sound management for his business. This meant that he could not tell when selling a house whether he made a profit or a loss. This was a recipe for disaster and during 1892 it became evident that William junior was unable to service his debts. By 31st October 1892 it had become obvious to William junior that he was insolvent and by the end of the year he was in Official Receivership. A final audit of the business was undertaken and it was clear that the excess of liabilities over assets amounted to £2,109. Mr E T Peirson, the Official Receiver, was critical of the fact that the books for the business were never kept accurately and that reckless trading had taken place. As the year 1892 came to an end William junior was declared bankrupt.

CHAPTER 38

William departs Royal Leamington Spa for Beckenham

The stigma attached to bankruptcy in Victorian society dictated that William senior could no longer reside in Royal Leamington Spa. In the spring of 1886 William and Martha decided to relocate to Beckenham, Kent, where William had received limited public exposure and where his son James had been the main representative for the Gascoyne business. The weather on the day for departure was overcast and gloomy, which matched the mood of the Gascoyne household in their Willes Road property. From early morning Martha stood in the bay window looking out to the road. Through her tear-filled eyes she observed the morning tradesmen making their deliveries. The muffled clink of metal caught her attention, and she noticed the milkman using his stainless steel ladle to measure quantities of milk from his churn into jugs presented to him each in turn by maids from the local households. She turned to her daughter Emily who was quietly observing her while sitting in a chair. "It's surprising how long you can live somewhere and still appreciate and miss the smallest daily events that go on around you," she uttered as her voice started to crack. As she finished speaking they heard the sound of a door opening and through the side window of the bay they noticed William junior and Gustavus carrying a trunk down the three sandstone steps from the front door. Martha realised the trunk contained the few possessions William had been allowed to retain by the court. She felt great sadness for her husband, knowing how much he had achieved in business and for his family and how he was affected by the loss.

William entered the room and came over to embrace his wife and said in a reassuring voice, "It's time for us to leave, dear." Martha shuddered and followed him outside without looking back. Their footsteps seemed to echo unusually loudly as they walked along the flagstone pavement to the waiting horse and carriage outside the front gate of the property. Despite the inclement weather, a small group of friends, neighbours and former employees had gathered to wish them well, and as they approached gave a spontaneous round of applause. William, who was not normally lost for words, found it hard to express his appreciation as he spoke in an emotional voice. "On behalf of my family, I would like to thank you from the bottom of my heart for your loyalty and friendship." William assisted Martha into the carriage and quickly followed. Once settled in his seat he banged on the ceiling as a signal to the driver to move off. A sudden rocking motion, accompanied by the sounds of a clinking bridle and the clattering of horse hooves, informed the couple that their journey had begun.

The carriage made its way along Warwick Street, turning left down the Parade towards the railway station. The sky became overcast and raindrops made a drumming sound on the carriage roof. The couple were in reflective mood as they travelled along the familiar main streets of the town containing examples of William's work. As William looked through the rain flecked glass of the carriage at the streets of his adopted town, he felt a great sadness as he realised that it was likely that he might never return. He knew that despite his absence there would always be a place in his heart for Royal

Leamington Spa, the town he loved so greatly. Martha was aware of William's hurt and sadness, but she was aware that there was nothing she could say or do to ease his pain.

As they arrived at Leamington railway station the rain abated. There was a distinct smell of coal smoke and oil in the atmosphere surrounding the couple as they sat on a wooden bench to await their train to take them to London. The journey to Beckenham, by way of the capital, was very familiar to William who had travelled it many times previously for business. On some occasions he had been accompanied by Martha who took the opportunity to see their grandchildren. However, unlike previous journeys when travelling in the relative luxury of a first-class carriage, on this occasion it was to be travelling in third class. The light was fading as they eventually arrived in Beckenham and they were greeted by a light drizzle of rain. As they travelled by carriage to their new home at Stanmore House, Southend Road, the couple's mood matched the depressing weather.

CHAPTER 39

William's final years

Once William and Martha were settled in at their new home in Beckenham, they were soon joined by their daughters. Their daughter Ann provided them with the good news that she intended to marry in September 1886. Her husband to be was Walter Tattersfield, the younger brother of her sister in law Annie. Walter, together with his father, was a fishmonger in Leamington who was well known to the Gascoyne family and who met with the full approval of both William and Martha. The couple chose to marry at St. Luke's parish church, Chelsea, in order that William and Martha would feel comfortable attending. Ann was delighted when her sister Juliet offered to sing at the wedding. It was widely agreed that William's youngest daughter Juliet was a talented singer with a sweet and admirably trained soprano voice which showed unmistakable evidence that she would succeed as a professional singer.

Despite the joy of her daughter Ann's wedding, William's faithful wife Martha pined for the family homes they had left in Warwickshire. William made every endeavour to pacify her, but with no success. Martha found it difficult to adapt to her new surroundings in Beckenham and was never able to settle into a happy and comfortable retirement. Three years after their relocation to Kent, Martha died aged sixty-four years old on 1st July 1889. In deference to her professed longing to return to Leamington, William and his family agreed that her body should be returned to Warwickshire for burial in the graveyard of St. Mary Magdalene parish church, Lillington. An emotional Juliet led the singing during the funeral service in a full capacity church prior to the internment of her coffin.

William expressed great pride and pleasure in following the singing career of his daughter. Juliet's reputation as a singer grew rapidly, but despite her success she never forgot the support and kindness her family were given by the people of her hometown. Soon after her mother's funeral she returned on Saturday 21st December 1889 to perform at the Leamington Town Hall for the Leamington Town Improvement Association concerts. Juliet was introduced as, "a native of Leamington, who since leaving the town has taken singing as a profession and studied in London where she has been very successful, having sung on different occasions at the Crystal Palace, St. James's Hall, and other important concerts."

Juliet returned to Leamington again in September 1891 to attend an illuminated promenade concert held in the Jephson Gardens on behalf of the Leamington Detachment of the Second Volunteer Battalion, Royal Warwickshire Regiment. The local newspaper reported, "A lovely autumnal evening induced a very large attendance and both the upper and lower gardens were promenaded during the evening by an animated throng. The two bands in attendance were the detachment band and the Town Improvement Association Band. The illuminated gardens presented an attractive scene with the lake encircled by chains of Japanese lanterns and fairy lamps besprinkled amongst the flower beds and the trees. The two bands were located in different ends of the gardens and played alternately. It was generally agreed that Miss Juliet Gascoyne's contribution was a most successful feature of the evening".

Sadly, one of the consequences of William junior's failed business activity was the forced sale of the Willes Road property. The house that had been a symbol of his father's success in business and a happy home for many years was vacated by members of the Gascoyne family for a final time in 1894. The premises were acquired for the office and yard of John Lewis, a timber merchant. William junior and his wife relocated to Wharfedale Street, Kensington, London, where he worked as an architect and surveyor. His youngest brother Gustave had married in 1891 and together with his family moved to Clerkenwell, London, where he obtained work as a building foreman.

William remained in Kent with his three daughters Elizabeth, Emily and Juliet in a modest residence in Manor Road, Beckenham. It was here that William received depressing news about the death of James, his oldest surviving son. After his arrival in Australia, James wandered from place to place for fifteen years around the state of Victoria drifting from one casual job to another. He lived on a poor diet and spent the majority of his free time in bars as his health declined. James was unable to break away from this unhealthy lifestyle, eventually submitting to its damaging physical affects, and he died aged forty-eight years old in Melbourne on 9th November 1897. It was a matter of continual regret for William that he and James were unable to resolve their differences and re-establish a good relationship before his son's death.

William, a lifelong devoted royalist, received the sad news that his greatly admired Queen Victoria had died on 22nd January 1901. For William this was yet one more unwelcome event in what seemed to be a succession of depressing events during recent years and caused him to become very melancholy and he suffered a marked lack of appetite. His daughters were devoted carers and nursed him during the following year as William became frail and suffered frequent periods of ill health. At the end of a particularly uncomfortable day on 9th October 1902, William's daughters wished him, "a comfortable night's sleep and the hope of a good day for tomorrow."

In a weak voice William responded in a positive manner, "Every day you wake up is a good day."

He did not wake up on the following morning. William's death at the age of seventy-six years was recorded on 10th October 1902.

News of William's demise was greeted with many expressions of regret. The report of his death in the *Beckenham Journal* outlined his significant contribution to the buildings in that town. An extensive account of his illustrious career was celebrated in his obituary printed in the *Leamington Courier*. The newspapers reported that William's burial at Elmers End Cemetery, Beckenham, was accompanied by, "many evidences of the respect in which the deceased was held, in the number of wreaths and letters sent, and places closed, and inhabitants present at the funeral".

The tragic circumstances surrounding the death of his first child due to poor sanitary provisions became the catalyst for William to become a lifelong champion for improvements in public health. It was therefore appropriate that he was buried in the same cemetery as Thomas Crapper, often cited as the person responsible for the flushing toilet becoming commonplace.

William's grave is marked by a modest cross headstone.

Printed in Great Britain
by Amazon